The Ragchild
Steve Lockley & Paul Lewis

The Ragchild

This book was first published in 2000 by
RazorBlade Press, 108 Habershon St, Splott,
Cardiff,
CF24 2LD

Designed and typeset by
RazorBlade Press

Printed and bound by the Guernsey Press.

British Library in Publication Data.
A catalogue record for this book is available
from the British Library

ISBN 0-9531468 2 0

INTRODUCTION

by Mark Chadbourne

WHAT maketh the man? Clothes? Not in this day-and-age where any old backstreet thug can pick up a nice whistle in which to secrete his razor-blade and anti-social behaviour. Genetics? For the sake of Fred West, Junior, let's hope not. How about the people who were around you when you were brought up?

Or how about where you were brought up?

I mention this because Steve Lockley and I grew up in the same area, went to the same school, dodged in and out of the same pubs when our elders weren't looking. And we both ended up with such a warped imagination and taste for the macabre it has dominated our lives. I make a living writing the kind of books Steve and I were told we shouldn't read at school. Steve has carved out a niche for himself as the author of some very creepy short stories and as an editor of the acclaimed anthology series, Cold Cuts, three nicely-packaged collections of shrieking nightmares.

And now this: his tour-de-force, The Ragchild.

Was it something in the South Derbyshire water that set the two of us down this dark path? Was it breathing in all that air blackened by the fumes from dark, Satanic pipe factories and coal dust belched up from mines that plumbed the borders of hell?

The truth is, every area has its own mythologies. Whispered in backstreet pubs and across market stalls, we hear accounts of the strange and unusual. Ghosts haunting mundane semis. Strange lights over power stations. Murderous tramps that hide in abandoned railway tunnels.

Stories shape our lives, and these were the ones that were floating around when Steve was a child, along with the regular yarns of the miners who populated our patch. People who live close to death all the time become very superstitious to help them deal with the omnipresent threat, and the miners, who spent all their time in constant shadow, had a particularly dark mythology.

From the evidence of The Ragchild, Steve also believes that places have power which mold those who live within their sphere. In this book you will find echoes of Fritz Leiber, another author who looked at a mundane scene and saw something very different from the rest of us. Something disturbing. Something that would make you want to move screaming to another place if you saw it.

The Ragchild is a story about the important of place, about the power that exists among the buildings, surging along the tarmac, creeping in the sewers. In its pages you will be transported to Swansea in South Wales, along streets, alleys and underpasses where you can walk any day. And then it will take a sharp detour to another Swansea, where terrors creep and the strange is commonplace. Swansea, you see, is Steve's home now and the place where he met his current collaborator, Paul Lewis, who also co-edited those wonderful Cold Cuts anthologies. They're both obviously cognizant with its moods and rhythms, its secret histories and brooding mythologies.

The Ragchild

Now I can't vouch for Paul's childhood, but I know he grew up in an area that might be geographically removed from Steve's home town, but which occupies the same space philosophically, intellectually and mythologically. What did Steve bring to this fine book, and what is Paul's? I have no idea, but that's one of the joys of The Ragchild. Their teaming is seamless; like minds, like hearts. I know Paul, like me, is a journalist by trade, a job which carries with it cynicism and romanticism in equal measures. And I know it's a job that leads you into the strangest places, down shadowy streets into hinterlands that most people never knew existed. Paul knows his people and knows his place, and I bet you he also knows lots of stories that never see print in the local rag. In The Ragchild you will hear them whisper about their city.

This Swansea is the kind of place you wouldn't want to go unless you had a very trusted guide. And Steve Lockley and Paul Lewis are the best guides of all. They know the alleys and by-ways, all those little stories that make a location come alive, and they won't leave you alone in the dark. Honest.

Be prepared to be hooked by their guide's spiel from the very beginning. You will quickly meet a range of believable characters, all dealing with their own particular crises. Who are they? What is the connection that links them? And what is the Ragchild? And then take your time getting to know the most intriguing character of all - the city itself. It lives and breathes and has its own personality. The Ragchild may not win any awards from the Swansea Tourist Board, but the rest of us will be thankful for having visited.

The Ragchild

For over the next few pages you will be introduced to wonders and fears, pain and heartache, joy and love and a mystery that will have you prowling your street looking for doors to *somewhere else*.

And you will also be privileged to be following two great writers into the next phase of their career, where their imagination is no longer restrained and their dreams have room to breathe. This is just the start, you see, and there are plenty more weird and wonderful places to visit.

Who knows? Maybe next time they will be dropping in to your home town. Come along...if you dare...

The Ragchild

ACKNOWLEDGEMENTS

Just a quick word of thanks to the following for their support: Darren Floyd, for accepting the novel on the basis of a few chapters; Mark Chadbourn for his perceptive introduction; Peter Crowther, Chaz Brenchley and Gary Greenwood for the kind words; and to XTC, (whose *Runaways* was the original inspiration), Mike Oldfield, Robert Miles and Vangelis for the musical accompaniment to the writing of The Ragchild.

-PROLOGUE-

The First Battle

Somewhere, something exploded. Maybe it was in his head, or maybe it was just close by. Then came the storm, and the sound of shelling mingled with the distant thunder. Each drop of rain splattered his face with mud, which felt freezing as it hit his skin. He pressed himself against the side of the trench but the deluge was impossible to avoid. Now that the sun had set it would start to get colder still.

There was only one escape: the thought of home. Of winter storms when black clouds would ride in from the sea as the gulls raced ahead of them. The smells of ozone and salt, the sounds of children running from the beach in search of shelter.

"You ready, son?" someone asked, jerking him back from there to the here and now. To the cold, the damp, the danger and the death.

"What?" Vaughan said, straining to hear.

"We're making our move. Our lads are trying to give us cover."

The shelling was aimed at positions the Germans had taken up. Another charge, another hill, another hundred yards gained which no doubt would be forfeited when the Kaiser's men returned fire. There seemed to be no winning. Only the pointless loss of men. Good men. Comrades and friends on each side.

"Well?" the officer demanded.

"Sir!" The word was repeated over and over right the way down the line as face after frightened face, many of them younger than Vaughan, gave the affirmation. At nineteen Vaughan had already served for almost two years. At the time he enlisted he had gladly lied about his age, proud to serve King and country. Now he was not so sure.

1

How many of those stood beside him would be alive by the time the sun rose again?

There was a momentary lull as the shelling stopped, then the sound of shouting in the distance, voices that carried in the near silence. Smoke and mist mingled, then drew closer to the ground before the pounding of artillery resumed.

"This is it, lads," said the officer, gripping the top rung of the trench ladder. Vaughan breathed hard. This could be his last few minutes of life. "Here we go."

And they went, running through smoke and gunfire, rifles before them with bayonets fixed. Around Vaughan soldiers fell with agonised cries. An explosion hurled him to the ground. He tasted wet earth, and then there was nothing.

"Can you hear me?" a voice whispered in his ear. Vaughan opened his eyes but all he could see were shapes blurred by the smoke.

"Hmm." He tried to speak but no words would form in his mouth.

"You just lie there, fella," said the voice. "Hang on."

Hang on? Hang on for what? Vaughan wanted to ask a whole host of questions but as he tried to raise his head he glimpsed bodies as far as the eye could see. He sank to the ground again. Hopeless. He tried to make out the face of the man who crouched beside him but could see nothing until a match burst temporarily into life. In that instant he saw the soft features of someone older than himself, one who seemed to possess a calmness in spite of the carnage around them. The man lit two cigarettes before blowing the match out. Never three on a light. The old superstition flashed across Vaughan's mind and a laugh escaped from his throat.

"That's the spirit," said the man, handing him one of the cigarettes. He was now lying beside Vaughan, no doubt to present a less likely target for the stray shots that rang out across the battlefield.

Vaughan wanted to tell him he didn't smoke and yet it did not seem to matter. Instead he breathed the smoke in deeply and coughed as his lungs burned. Pain lanced through his shoulder and for the first time he realised he had been shot.

"Don't worry," said the stranger. "I have to check on a few others but I'll come back for you as soon as it's dark." He pushed another couple of Woodbines into the top pocket of Vaughan's tunic, then placed a water flask on the ground beside him.

The smoke caught in Vaughan's eyes, making them water. By the time his vision cleared the stranger had gone. All he could see around him were the dead and the dying. He took a second draw on the cigarette, then another. Slowly the taste began to block out the taste of cordite, something he knew he would always remember.

He must have drifted off to sleep, though he could not recall closing his eyes. When he woke it was nearly dark again. The groans from the injured had diminished, though he could still hear the occasional feeble cry. When he tried to move, the pain in his shoulder was too much to bear and he had to hold on against a drowning sensation.

A shape walked towards him, ignoring the threat of sniper fire. "Still here?" it said. A man, though not the one who had come to Vaughan before. The voice was older, deeper, confident to the point of arrogance.

"Hanging on," he answered.

"Good."

Vaughan was uneasy. This man felt like no saviour. Where was the other one? Why hadn't he come back, as he'd promised? Vaughan looked around but there was no movement and no sound. No cries of pain, no gunshots, no shelling. He would have cried out for help but sensed there was no one close enough to hear him.

"No point," the man said, as if reading Vaughan's mind. "No point at all. Sometimes the distance between here and there is further than you think."

"And sometimes it's much closer," another voice called from out of the mist. A friendly voice. The cigarette man.

"This is not your place."

"Nor is it yours," said the cigarette man. "This is no man's land."

"Then he does not belong here, either."

"True, true. And that is why I am here. To take him home."

"Whose home? His or yours?"

"Maybe they are the same."

"Unlikely, I think," said the older man, his tone menacing, leaving Vaughan more afraid than he had ever felt in battle. "He would be better with me."

"Do I have a choice?" Vaughan asked, finding the words at last, feeling like a helpless bystander caught in the middle of a dispute over property.

"None whatsoever," said the older man. "Some things are beyond the understanding of ordinary people."

"What do you mean, ordinary people?" Vaughan snapped. "Aren't those who fought here, no matter which side they are on, just ordinary people?"

"Maybe on your battlefield," said the man, waving his arm in the direction of the dead who now seemed some distance away even though Vaughan still lay in exactly the same place. "But not on ours."

Vaughan raised himself to one elbow, no longer feeling the pain in his shoulder. "What does he mean?" he asked the cigarette man.

"It doesn't concern you. This is between him and me. Between dark and light. Between those who want change and those who want the world to stay the same."

"And which side are you on?" Vaughan asked, convinced now that he was experiencing some kind of delirium brought on by his injuries.

"I am on the side of those who wish to keep things as they are. As are you."

"I am?" Vaughan did not understand a word of this. Either both men were talking gibberish or, if they were indeed phantoms, his own mind was rambling.

"He stays with me," said the older man. "This one, this time."

"No. I'm taking him home."

"Are you going to stop me?"

"If I have to."

"And do you think you are strong enough to defeat me?"

"Maybe not. But I know I can stop you for at least a while."

A snort of derision.

"And you think that is enough?"

"Enough to make sure that he can leave this place."

"But at what cost?" The older man's voice began to rise. His eyes started to bulge and the veins at his temples throbbed and protruded.

"To me or to you? I will pay whatever it costs. Are you prepared to do the same?"

But instead of replying the older man seemed to lurch into uncontrollable rage. The features of his face ran like liquid, blurring and reshaping as if layers of flesh were boiling off in turn to reveal others beneath.

"The real you?" the cigarette man asked as the final layers peeled away to leave a boy standing there. A boy who to Vaughan seemed more menacing and dangerous than anyone who had ever held a gun.

"The real me," the boy said. "No more pretending."

A boy. That's all he was. A boy standing in the middle of all this death and destruction and yet somehow apart from it. A boy, but not a boy. The cigarette man took a St Christopher's medal from his neck and placed it around Vaughan's.

"Your ticket home," he said. "A kind of talisman. Remember, sometimes the distance between two places is not quite as far as it seems."

Then he turned and walked towards the boy, his arms held wide. The child welcomed him with a laugh that was hideously inhuman and that Vaughan thought would never end. It echoed around Vaughan's brain until he felt like screaming, but then darkness swooped over him and carried him away in its merciful embrace.

ONE

Long Tom strode through the streets of Old Town. It was morning but early, the August sun too weak to entirely banish the night. A chill breeze sent litter cascading across the cracked and weed-choked roads and created small dust devils which died within moments of birth. Tom's unbuttoned khaki trench coat, an integral part of his attire for so many years that he had been named for it, flapped around his heels before rising into the air like a bird taking flight. He wrestled the contrary garment back into place, holding it still with a belt which he twisted and tied round his narrow waist. Throughout this manoeuvre he did not break his stride. He had business to do and did not want to be late. That was not his style.

Arriving at a crossroads that had once been at the heart of the city, Tom halted and glanced at his watch. Nine-thirty. He shrugged. It had shown nine-thirty every time he had looked at it for the past half-century or more. Some habits were hard to break, he guessed. He leaned against the rust-riddled shutter of a shop which had ceased trading long before the Luftwaffe dropped its bombs, and waited. He placed a cigarette between his lips, lighting it with a match which he ignited by flicking his thumbnail up against its head one of his favourite Western movie tricks.

Smoke filled his lungs and he held it in for a moment before exhaling it in a long, satisfied stream. Damn, that felt good. Then again, in this place smoking always felt good. No guilt. And no cancer. Old Town saw to that, like it saw to everything else.

Tom looked at his watch again. Nine-thirty. Tinker was late. No matter. Tom had all the time in the world. He sat on the cold pavement, back against the shutter, and waited. There were few people about this early, and most of them paid him no attention. A few nodded as they passed. Long Tom said nothing in return, just smiled and smoked, lighting his second cigarette from the smoldering butt of the first. He liked this time of day almost as much as he enjoyed solitude, welcomed the chance to put his thoughts in order in preparation for dealing with the trials and tribulations of life. Most of all he enjoyed watching the sun come up over forgotten buildings, feeling the place come alive as the city aroused from its slumber. The buildings across the way from him appeared dead. Their boarded-up windows were like the unseeing eyes of the blind, but Tom knew there were memories burning behind each broken facade. Nothing was ever lost in Old Town. What had been always would be, Long Tom included.

A dishevelled figure turned a corner and appeared on the street before him. Its clothes were little more than rags, held together by a few stitches and a lot of good luck. It shuffled slowly along the pavement, swaying slightly, an old leather bag clutched in both hands, wheezing as it walked. Tom lit his third cigarette and watched the figure's progress impassively. By the time it reached him there was nothing left of his cigarette but its stub and the tar in his lungs. Tom stood, yawning, then waited in silence while Tinker placed the bag on the ground and snapped open its clasp. The arthritic old trader groaned slightly as he straightened.

"And how are ya today, Long Tom?" he said by way of greeting.

"Same as ever," Tom said. "Getting by."

Tinker sniffed loudly, wiping the back of a grimy hand across his nose. "For a man who lacks nothing you can be a miserable bastard at times. No offence meant."

Tom winked. None taken. "Lacking nothing ain't the same as wanting nothing. I'd rather have nothing and be content than want too much and end up disappointed. "

"I come here to trade and all I get is bullshit," Tinker complained to the sky.

"So," said Tom, crouching beside the bag, "let's see what you have for me."

Within a minute he had placed the results of Tinker's scavenging in a semicircular arrangement on the pavement. Most of it was junk: cheap jewellery, a wallet which was both battered and empty, a screwdriver; a tube of suntan lotion. These Tom put back into the bag almost without a glance. Then he pondered what remained: a pair of gold pince-nez spectacles and a handful of coins. "Ain't much," he said.

Tinker shrugged. "You could always try finding this stuff for yourself."

"That, my friend, is what people like you are for." Tom tapped a finger against his chin. "Okay. I'll take what's there. Subject, of course, to your quoting a fair price."

"Two bottles."

Long Tom merely stared at him, one eyebrow raised.

"Coins could be worth a bit," Tinker persisted.

"One bottle."

"There's others out there who'll pay a lot — "

"One bottle. Take it or leave it."

"Oh, all right, all right," Tinker said unhappily. "One it is."

Tom removed a bottle from an inside pocket of his coat and

handed it to Tinker, who unscrewed the cap and raised the neck to his lips before downing several fingers of whisky. The old trader gasped, nodded appreciatively, then offered the bottle to his companion, who shook his head. "Just the one bad habit for me," Tom said, going about the business of lighting his fourth cigarette.

"Suit yourself," Tinker said, taking another long drink. He looked quizzically at Tom. "Always meant to ask. What do you do with all that stuff you buy, anyway?"

"Find a home for it. People will pay a lot for antiques."

"Antiques?" Tinker laughed. "Load of old junk lying about the place waiting to be picked up by the likes of me, that's all it really is. And you know it, Long Tom."

"Yes, *I* know it," Tom conceded. "But they don't."

They said nothing else for a while, each man taking the time to savour his preferred vice, understanding it could not do him any harm. By now the air had grown pleasantly warm. It inspired the city to stir. A few of the more enterprising inhabitants emerged, from the homes they had made in the time-worn buildings, to go about their business of the day. Most of them ignored the two men standing on the cross-roads. Besides, they were inclined to steer clear of Long Tom, especially when he was buying. That was the way he liked it, and word got around quickly in this place. If a man wanted to be left alone, you left him alone.

Tinker raised the whisky bottle to his lips one final time and looked with an almost sorrowful expression at its depleted contents. He screwed the cap back on and placed the bottle with exaggerated care into his bag. "That's enough for now," he said. "Got things to take care of. Be around in a couple of days, if you're interested."

"I'm always interested," Tom said. "You should know that."

"Aye." Tinker turned to leave, then hesitated. "Tell me, Tom. You ever wake up in the morning feeling, you know, just the slightest bit worried about all this?"

"I never wake up in the morning," said Tom. "I never sleep."

"Yeah, well, you know what I mean." Tinker looked uncomfortable, as if he guessed he was asking questions of Long Tom that had never been asked before. "I mean, this place, it's our home and everything, but sometimes I can't help wonder ..."

"Wonder what?"

"If maybe we're just a little too set in our ways."

Tom flicked his cigarette away, watching tiny sparks fly off it as the breeze snatched it up and sent it bouncing and skittering along the road. "This is the life we chose when we accepted the city."

"Don't get me wrong," Tinker said quickly. "I'm not knocking it. Christ, Tom, I've lived here eighty years now, longer even than you, but I still can't get used to the fact that every single day is exactly the same as the another. Sometimes I wonder if my eighty years is like a blink of an eye to the city. I can't help thinking that maybe tomorrow I'll wake up to find all this gone and something else in its place."

"Nothing will change," Tom said.

"How can you be sure about that?"

"I'm sure. Believe me."

"Well," Tinker said. "I hope you're right, my friend. Because if there was any kind of change I'm not sure we'd be able to adapt. We're too set in our ways." And with that he nodded at Tom, who nodded back, then shuffled away down the street.

Tom watched him go before setting off in the opposite direc-

11

tion, slowly, deep in thought. He got on well enough with Tinker but the old fella was borderline crazy and not usually given to profundity. Yet what he had said about change nagged at Tom, who had long harboured his own concerns about the relationship between the city and those who lived within its peculiar boundaries. It was kind of symbiotic but not, he felt sure, in any way that nature had intended.

Swearing under his breath, Tom rummaged in his pockets until he had found his cigarettes and, lighting one, forced his mind to concentrate on the matter at hand. He had saleable goods. It was time for him to make his first trip to the outside world for several months. Long Tom regarded the prospect with resignation rather than anticipation. He never ventured outside unless he had to. However, he had to admit, this was one such occasion. Tom was short of cigarettes and books, the twin loves of his life. Nothing else for it, he thought. Soon he was following the twisting network of forgotten alleyways and hidden turnings which took him out of Old Town.

TWO

Kelvin Denny held the small gold frame in his left hand and with the thumb of his right brushed softly over the face of the baby which beamed back at him. There were no tears on the child's face that needed wiping away, yet there could so easily be on his own. He knew it would only take a momentary lapse in his resolve for the floodgates to open. They said time healed everything, but his grief was still raw even after six months. He was constantly aware of it, a cancerous emptiness eating away at him from within.

"Where are you, Jessica?" he whispered.

There was a tap on his office door and he quickly put the photograph back down on his desk as if caught in an act that he should be ashamed of, then rubbed a knuckle under each eye. The door opened before he had a chance to compose himself. Kelvin felt a twinge of annoyance. You didn't just barge straight into the boss's office. You waited until you were told to enter. He almost barked a reprimand but it died on his lips when he saw it was Tanya. Almost at once he felt the tide of sadness ebb a little.

"Coffee?" said the face with a smile that made him forget so much of his pain.

"Thanks," he said, anxiously peering over Tanya's shoulder as she put a mug down on a coaster at the edge of his desk. She must have noticed his concern.

"Don't worry. Everyone is either having a break or tied up with a customer."

"Right," he said nervously. The bank was a hotbed of gossip, and he wanted to avoid sparking a rumour that he and Tanya were lovers. Not that they *were* lovers. Not really.

"So when do *I* get tied up?" she giggled.

"Sorry?" he said raising the mug of steaming coffee to his lips.

"Just wondering when I could ... you know ... see you again."

"You're seeing me now, aren't you?"

She moved closer, resting one hand on the desk. "I meant see you properly."

"I don't know," he said. "Perhaps tomorrow."

"What's wrong with tonight?"

"Mary. We're supposed to be seeing friends."

"So you'd rather be with her." She jutted out her lower lip in mock hurt. It was a childlike gesture. Then again, he reminded himself, Tanya was little more than a child.

"That's not what I'm saying. It's just difficult. With Jessica and everything. And there are not many friends who haven't got fed up with the whole thing and drifted away."

"God, Kelvin, I'm sorry. I never thought."

That was the problem. She never thought. Nothing mattered to her, except having a good time. Still, he loved to be with her. Somehow her energy gave him the strength to cope with everything that was going on around him. He could listen to the slight giggle in her voice for hours and not tire of it, and feel the warmth and softness of her skin from inches away. So far she had been happy just sitting and talking in his car, listening to the sound of the sea washing against the docks, or looking out across the headland to the Mumbles lighthouse. But sooner or later things would change. Kelvin worried it might not be for the better. Sometimes when things changed they spoiled, turned rotten, leaving a bitter taste behind even when you were remembering the good times.

He knew he should let her go, tell Tanya she was too young, that she could do a lot better than him, tell her anything that would put her out of his reach and beyond temptation. But he could not. He would look at her face, marvel at her startlingly blue eyes, recall the sudden thrill which ran through him like an electric shock each time her hand had brushed against his as they sat in the car. He could not let her go. And it was not as if he was cheating on Mary, for Christ's sake. He and Tanya were just friends. All the same, he was aware it had the potential to go further. Much further. Deep down he wanted it to, knowing that it would make him a shit of the first order after what had happened with Jessica but not really caring. Mary had her way of dealing with it. And he had his.

The telephone on his desk rang suddenly, jarring him back to normality.

"Yes?"

"Sorry to disturb, Mr Denny. Call for you."

"Who is it, Sylvia?" He was glad of the interruption, but surprised he had not heard the telephone ring in the outer office. Surprised, and a little worried. He had to be aware of everything that was going on — how many people were waiting to be served, how many cashiers could be called on at any time, how long it took for the phone to be answered. The three-ring circus. Although he should be able to let other people worry about such mundane activities, he knew he must remain attentive. Duties apart, he could so easily alert others to his and Tanya's less-than-formal relationship if he allowed his concentration to slip.

15

"It's the police," Sylvia said matter-of-factly.

"About anyone in particular?" A call from the police was not uncommon. At any given time there could be half a dozen cases going on which he needed to deal with, everything from simple cheque-book misuse to suspected money-laundering transactions.

"He wouldn't say."

"Okay. Put him through," he said, heart suddenly racing. Did they have news about Jessica? He forced a smile into place for Tanya, who had already moved to the doorway, and cupped his hand over the receiver. "Speak to you later," he whispered.

Then, into the phone: "Kelvin Denny. How can I help you?"

"Mr Denny, this is Detective Sergeant Miles, Swansea CID."

"Is it about Jessica?"

"Jessica? No, it's about your wife."

For a moment Kelvin did not grasp what he was hearing, then the words hit him with the force of a hammer blow. Please God, not Mary. For all his thoughts of betrayal, he knew he would be lost if anything happened to her. First his daughter, then his wife.

"Is she okay?" he said, not knowing if he wanted to hear the answer.

"Your wife is fine," said the detective. "She's here in the station."

Kelvin slumped with relief. "Then what's the matter?"

"It would be better if you could come here. I'd ... I'd rather explain in person."

"I'll be straight round," Kelvin said, glancing instinctively at his watch.

"Thank you, sir." The line clicked and went dead.

It was the height of summer and the city had seen its share of tourists in the last few weeks. Today, though The Kingsway was fairly quiet. Perhaps this was the day for visitors to explore the Gower beaches. A few early lunchers sat at the plastic tables on the street outside one of the bistros as if they were on the Continent, rather than a couple of yards away from a road where traffic roared past almost constantly.

Kelvin took the steps down to the underpass at a jog. A solitary musician was plying his trade with a tin whistle, on which he played spirited Irish folk tunes and played them rather well.. Beyond him, two drunks with cans of Special Brew propped each other up on one of the benches in the open space in the centre. "Spare us a quid, boss?" one asked as Kelvin approached. He ignored the man, but made a mental note to drop some change in the inverted baseball cap the musician had placed on the pavement. He did not mind giving money to someone who was trying to earn it, rather than simply accosting passers by. Assuming he came back the same way to the office. It was hardly important but Kelvin needed something to take his mind off Mary. And Jessica.

"I said, can you spare us a quid?" The man was overtly aggressive this time, rising unsteadily to his feet and placing one filthy hand on Kelvin's shoulder.

"No," Kelvin said, looking at the hand, feeling its grip tighten on his jacket.

"You sure?"

Kelvin could see the second drop-out put his can down and watch the exchange with gleeful interest. Should threat turn to violence there was no doubt he would join in. Great. That was all he

17

needed, two pissheads trying to mug him now of all times.

"You sure?" the aggressive man repeated.

The blast of foul breath made Kelvin flinch more than the thinly veiled threat, and he looked into the man's heavily bloodshot eyes. "Yes," he said. He briefly considered fishing in his pockets for a few coins just so he could get to the police station, although he was certain small change would not satisfy this pair. But then, without warning, the drunk let go and stared at one of the other underpass openings. Kelvin felt his gaze drawn in the same direction.

Standing framed by the entrance to the tiled concrete tunnel was a tall, gaunt man. He wore a long khaki coat despite the heat, and was watching the exchange without an expression on his face. But his eyes ... there was something, a blankness, which sent a chill running through Kelvin. They were the eyes of a dead man, or of a man who had been so close to death for so long that it had clouded the windows of his soul.

The drunk slumped back onto the bench beside his companion and Kelvin hurried on, thankful for this strange wordless intervention. He looked back just before he stepped into the shadow of the passage that led up to Orchard Street, but the gaunt figure had gone and the drunks were once again giving the Special Brew cans their full attention.

-THREE-

It hurt to move. Pain ripped through his side every time he shifted. He lay as still as he could, flat on his back on the rock-hard floor which was so cold he thought he must surely freeze to death. This was not working out the way he had thought. He was alone and more than a little afraid. It wasn't kind of fear he got from reading a Stephen King book or watching a horror movie. This was real- life scary. Like watching your mother die when you were too young to understand why. Like lying in bed with a feeling of dread every night as the old man staggered in drunk and itching for a fight.

This last thought made Martyn realise that his situation was not completely hopeless after all. The pain would fade in time. The cold would go when the sun rose. And the old man would never find him here even if he could be bothered to look. Fat chance of that, Martyn thought. As far as he could tell, his father thought of him as little more than his own personal punchbag, someone he could use to take out his anger and frustration.

Pain flared up in his ribs again, as if his thoughts had reminded them of the beating they had taken just a couple of days ago. Drink had started that one off, like it had all the others before it. These days the old man seemed unable to do anything other than prop up the bar in the Globe, that and lash out at Martyn whenever he felt like it. He would spend most of the afternoon and all night knocking back pint after pint, short after short, all of it paid for by the insurance money they'd got when Mum died. Then he would stagger home and start a fight over the stupidest little thing, and it always ended with Martyn bruised and in tears.

19

But not any more, he thought. Not any more.

The car park was an enormous cavern in the dark. Martyn had waited until the last of the commuters and shoppers had driven off, leaving the place deserted. Then he had searched about until he found an area beneath a stairwell on the fourth level that looked reasonably well hidden, just in case there were any security guards on patrol. Finally he had zipped himself inside his tattered old sleeping bag and, using his rucksack as a pillow, tried to get to sleep.

That had been two hours ago. He was still wide awake.

The pain had a lot to do with it. The last time his father had beaten him, the reason why he had finally decided to take control of his life by running away, Martyn had felt something give in his right side. He assumed one of his ribs was broken. It still hurt, agonisingly so, every time he moved. All he could do was hope that it healed quickly and of its own accord. He could not risk going to the hospital. Anyone who saw him there would see he was just a kid. They would call the police, who in turn would take him back home, and then the shit would really hit the fan. Martyn knew the pain he was feeling now would be nothing compared to how he would feel once the police had gone, leaving him at his father's mercy.

Stuff that, he thought.

He had no intention of going home again. Ever. Despite all he had been through, it had not been easy, making the decision to leav, giving up his friends and his dog and all the familiar little things he saw in and around the house every day of his life. He wondered if he would ever stop missing them, whether he would ever become used to this new life he had chosen for himself. He doubted it. Sleeping on the floor of a multi-storey car park was ... well, it wasn't what he was used to. Distant traffic, the horns of the ships in Swansea Bay, even the whisper of the summer breeze, each sound seemed so different in the open. At least the last of the trains seemed to have left the station alongside the car park.

Martyn knew there were things he would have to start thinking about if he was going to survive living rough. Stupid things, like washing his clothes, cleaning his teeth, even what to do with himself every day with no school, no friends and no home to go to. He had been to Swansea before, loads of times, and had been bored after a couple of hours. Now he was living there. He had the horrible feeling that every day was going to feel like life in prison. He was aware he would have to be careful with the money he had brought with him, would have to make it last for some time until he could find some way of managing without it. And he would manage, he promised himself, even if that took a while. He had to be positive. He had no other choice.

Then there was finding somewhere to sleep each night. He doubted he could risk using the car park as a permanent home. Someone was bound to spot him, sooner or later. Okay, so finding somewhere else was a priority. Tomorrow, though. For now he just wanted to lie still enough for the pain to go and allow sleep to take him away.

It had all been so easy to begin with. Leaving early while the old man was still sleeping off his latest hangover, walking the few miles from Cwmavon to Port Talbot, catching the bus to Swansea. He'd wandered the streets for a while, the August sun making him a lot more cheerful than he had felt for some time. When the light had started to fade he began to search for somewhere to sleep, remembering the car park near the station from years ago when his mother had taken him shopping for the day.

21

Life wasn't fair. Otherwise his mother would be alive, his father dead.

Sadness and exhaustion overwhelmed him. He slept. Fitfully, but he slept.

There were hands on him when he woke. Martyn blinked in the sunlight, for a moment too confused to understand what was happening. Then everything fell into place. A man was kneeling over him, face a map of red veins, eyes like a vampire's. He had pulled the sleeping bag from Martyn and was hurriedly searching his pockets.

"Get off me!" Martyn yelled, trying to hit the hand away. It was useless.

"Shut your fucking trap," the man hissed, his breath a wave of alcohol. "Just give us some fucking money and I won't have to hurt you, all right?"

Martyn squirmed away from him. "I haven't got any money."

"Like fuck," said the man, pulling open the rucksack and searching through its contents. "Kids always got fucking money. Don't like sharing, though, oh no."

He suddenly grinned, and pulled out a small black wallet. "What's this, then?"

"Give that back!" Martyn made a grab for it.

The man jerked it out of his way, then stood and began rifling through the folded notes inside. He looked down at Martyn and shook his head sadly. "Naughty boy. Lying to me like that. Must be, I don't know, forty, fifty quid in here."

"It's all I've got. Please, let me have it."

"Let you have it ..." the man said, as if deep in thought. And then, with a speed he did not look capable of, he kicked Martyn in the side. White hot pain flared in the boy's ribs, so immense it eclipsed everything else. He moaned, writhing, tasting blood in his mouth from where he had bitten his tongue. Martyn had not felt that, just as he did not feel the second kick, this one catching him on the hip. "That'll teach you to fucking lie," he heard as if from a great distance, and then there was nothing.

-FOUR-

The place seduced him. Every time he returned he was swept away by its bustle and energy, its sounds, its smells, so different from the timeless calm in which he spent most of his days. Old Town was home but Long Tom still felt himself drawn to Swansea, even though it had changed almost beyond recognition since his childhood.

He came back when he had to and stayed only for as long as was necessary. Not because he was in any rush to leave. Quite the opposite. Tom was addicted to the city's vitality, but at the same time was constantly aware that every hour spent there was an hour stolen from his life. Old Town could not reverse the ageing process, only suspend it. Neither was he protected from illness or injury. He was as vulnerable as any man, and he did not care for the way that made him feel.

As the years passed Tom had fallen into a routine. He would make his way to whichever antique shop he was currently doing business with, and take what money he could before stocking up with cigarettes and whisky and books. Then he would go straight back to where he felt he belonged. No detours. No distractions. Most of all, he would not allow himself to become involved with anything or anyone. The world may be a continually evolving source of fascination, but it did not outweigh his overriding desire to stay alive. Old Town offered immortality, and that was something Tom was not about to spurn. A man who lived forever could savour the world in his own time.

The trinkets that Tinker had sold to him, together with those he had found for himself, were a comforting weight in his trench coat pocket. It was mid-morning and the sun had begun to rise above the city centre buildings. Heat made the tarmac shimmer in front of him but Tom did not feel unduly warm. In fact, he never felt unduly anything. He was never cold, hot, tired or hungry. His body was like a well-tuned engine ticking over, even when he left Old Town. Maybe the place's protective influence continued to shield him after he passed beyond its boundaries. Tom did not know, nor did he particularly care.

He emerged from the lane which separated this world from Old Town and was immediately surrounded by an endless stream of people, all rushing by with the same expression on their faces, a look that seemed close to panic. Beyond them cars and buses filled the air with unnatural sounds and toxic fumes, making it unpalatable even to Tom's smoke-tainted lungs. Across the road was Castle Gardens, no longer the green oasis of his childhood. Gone were the trees and much of the grass, replaced with paving slabs and a wide sweep of amphitheatre-style steps on which sprawled dozens of youths. A cascade led down to a circular fountain. Tom could hear the hiss of its spray above the roar of traffic and the babble of voices around him. The gardens were overlooked by a tower block whose windows snared the sunlight and threw it back as pure dazzling white. It dwarfed what remained of the castle, which saddened him. The ruins were the city's sole surviving link with its ancient self, yet they were so insignificant that hardly anyone so much as glanced at them as they hurried along.

He sighed and started walking along Princess Way, passing the McDonald's with a grimace of distaste before turning left into the writhing mass of humanity that was Oxford Street. Tom took a deep breath and cut a path through the teeming crowd, which obligingly parted before him. Maybe it was his height or his old and grubby long coat or the intolerant look on his face. Whatever it was, something about him apparently made people want to step smartly out of his way. That brought a grin to Tom's face, the pleasing realization that for some reason or another, and without even trying, he intimidated those who lived in Swansea as much as the sheer number of them intimidated him.

He heard the shouts as he drew close to Marks and Spencer. Without intending to he glanced towards the storefront, where two women appeared to be grappling over a small bright parcel which each was trying to wrestle from the other, screeching abuse as they did so. Beside them was a pram. Tom realised with a sudden sense of disbelief that what they were fighting over was not a parcel, but a baby. He stumbled to a halt and watched as a man grabbed one of the women, a blonde, and pushed her roughly up against one of the glass doors. The other woman hugged the baby to her chest and began to rock on her heels. By now a small crowd had gathered around the combatants, regarding the extraordinary tableau before them with the same mute astonishment as that felt by Long Tom. Seconds later a policeman appeared on the scene, conjured as if by magic. He spoke to the man before putting a hand on the blonde's elbow. A policewoman jogged up from behind Tom and briefly conferred with her colleague. Then she spoke to the blonde who, judging by the violent shaking of her head and the equally fierce look on her face, obviously disagreed with whatever the policewoman had said.

The blonde's remonstrations had no effect. Lips pursed, the policewoman used both hands to turn her around and snapped a pair of handcuffs over her wrists with uncanny speed. At this point the woman fell silent. Her head slumped and she looked like all the fight had gone out of her, as instantly as if a switch had been flicked. But as the policewoman began to lead her away she glanced up and her eyes met Tom's. Fleetingly, and probably coincidentally, but even so a shudder of recognition ran through him at the moment of contact. He was convinced he knew her, even though he was equally certain he had never met her before. In her eyes was a look of such profound despair that Tom wanted to intervene, to say or do anything to help, an impulse he had to struggle to resist. Never get involved, he told himself. Let other people look after their own problems.

And so he turned on his heels and started walking, whispering an apology to the woman. Guilt nagged at Tom as he strode towards St Helen's Road, but he shrugged it off. There was nothing he could have done. Nothing. Okay, so he felt bad about it now. Of course he did. He was not a bad man. He had a conscience. But give it a couple of hours and he'd have forgotten all about her. Or at least that's what he made himself think. It was easier that way.

St Helen's Road was an oasis of calm after Oxford Street. It was on the edge of the city centre and pleasantly unfashionable. None of the superstores here. Just a long row of shops, each with its own character, mingling happily with the occasional Asian restaurant, launderette and taxi office. "Yesteryears" was roughly halfway along. It was, like its neighbours, undistinguished, almost shabby, with a display window full of what its owner believed were, or at least tried to pass off as, antiques. Tom knew better. It was junk. The trinkets he carried in his pockets were probably worth more than the entire display. Still, you could hardly blame the man for trying. If something looked old enough or battered enough, some fool would be willing to pay good money for it.

When Tom emerged into the sunshine again only a few minutes later his pockets were lighter, his wallet fuller. He began retracing his steps to the city centre, picking up his pace as he drew nearer. He had been out of Old Town for more than an hour and he was itching to get back. First, though, he had a few stops to make. He crossed the busy roundabout to The Kingsway and called in at Tesco, stocking up with packs of cigarettes for himself as well as the whisky he would use to pay Tinker next time. Then he headed for a discount bookshop which sold imported Western paperbacks from America at a fraction of the price he'd pay elsewhere. In total, Tom spent maybe a quarter of the money he had earned from the trip. Not a bad day out, all told. He had plenty left over, enough to finance a few expeditions into the outside world without having to go to the trouble of foraging or bargaining with Tinker.

By now the streets were even busier than they had been earlier, if that were possible, and the traffic was virtually bumper-to-bumper. Exhaust gases mixed with the stagnant atmosphere to produce a sepia haze which hung unpleasantly in the air. Tom wondered how people tolerated it, why they didn't just head for the beach or the countryside on days like today and leave the city until winter when you could at least breathe without almost choking. He took the steps to the subway beneath the Oxford Street roundabout at a trot, feeling more anxious than ever to get home. The tiled walls of the underpass echoed back the quick-fire click of his boots until he emerged into the sunken garden at the open centre of the roundabout. A few years ago you could have sat on one of the benches here and soaked up some sunshine in peace. No longer. The place, like too many others, had been taken over by the down-and-outs, the heavy drinkers, the drug addicts. Even at this relatively early hour most of the benches had already been claimed by men dressed in little more than rags, their faces grimy, their eyes blank, their expressions either vacant or menacing.

Over the din of the traffic which thundered above him, Tom could hear music, thin and reedy but lively nonetheless. He paused a moment while he tried to locate its source. Then just inside the mouth of the subway tunnel, he spotted a young man, fingers dancing along a tin whistle. At his feet a baseball cap held a sprinkling of coins which reflected the light in tiny sunbursts. Damn, he played well. Tom closed his eyes a moment, enjoying the Celtic tune the young man was playing with a verve and ability that belied his age. It had been a long time since Tom had heard music like that, and longer still since he had heard it played with such panache. He reached into his pocket for change, pulling out a fistful of coins which he reckoned amounted to four or five pounds. Tom decided to give it all to the musician, who deserved every penny in his cap and far more, but for now he just wanted to stand and listen, relishing the images the sound conjured up.

As he was standing there, lost in the past, hand tapping lightly against his leg in time with the music, Tom saw a well-dressed man pass by the musician, not quite running but certainly in a hurry. The man emerged into sunlight, blinking, and stumbled to a halt, looking around as if unsure of his bearings. One of the derelicts, a grubby fellow with a thick dark beard, looked up from his bench and said something. Either there was no answer or the derelict did not like the response, for he immediately staggered upright and put his hand on the man's shoulder. Tom watched carefully. Helping a woman who had broken the law, with plenty of police around, would only have brought trouble down on himself. This was different. It was ... what?

29

The Ragchild

Tom shook his head, confused. Why was it different? He felt as though someone else's thoughts had been inside his head. He simply did not get involved with others. Ever. Without warning the derelict let go of the man and stared directly at Tom. Tom held the derelict's stare until the other looked away, spitting at the ground in apparent disgust.

The man in the suit seemed rooted to the spot. *Best get out of here*, Tom willed him. He went to resume his own journey, but suddenly realised he felt strangely uncomfortable at the prospect of crossing the gardens. God knew why. Tom did not consider himself a violent man, but he was capable of violence and would not hesitate to defend himself, and defend himself well, if he had to. Still, something felt wrong. His visits to Swansea usually passed without incident. This time he had witnessed an attempted baby-snatch and, without knowing how, had broken up a fight in the making. All that in the space of two hours. Ah well. Maybe it was just going to be one of those days. Deciding to follow his instincts, which had never let him down before, Tom turned and retraced his steps out of the subway, back to the crushing tide of humanity and the never-ending roar of traffic.

He reached Princess Way without further incident, passing the McDonald's and turning into the lane behind it, halfway along which lay his path to Old Town. He was now relieved to be back on what already felt like home turf. And that was when he saw them: three men, dressed in the ragged clothes of the dispossessed, two holding down a boy who was years younger than them, the third administering a ferocious beating. Tom almost groaned. He'd had enough trouble for one day. All he wanted was to finish the short journey home, smoke his cigarettes, read the first of his Westerns. For some reason, though, fate or the gods or whatever the hell else it was that controlled his destiny was hell-bent on holding him up. Well, he was not going to go along with it.

There was no way home from here; the gate through which he had emerged was now closed. In its place was a solid brick wall. Old Town concealed itself from strangers and from trouble. No problem. All he had to do was find another quiet part of the city and wait for Old Town to reveal itself to him. The problem was, he could not tear his eyes away from the scene before him. *Don't get involved*, he told himself. *Just turn around, find another way back.* Yeah, sure. Like he could just walk away from this. Tom had no idea what that kid had done wrong but, whatever it was, surely to God it could not possibly warrant such brutal retribution.

Tom sized up the three men. The one delivering the punches was tall and rangy but what he might lack in bulk he was making up for in grim determination. His two cohorts were crouched over the supine boy, pinning down his arms, and while they seemed shorter they also appeared far more solid than the first. Tom glanced along the lane but there was no one about. Of course not. The three had a look about them which suggested they were no strangers to trouble. They would have made certain they were unobserved before they started punishing the boy for whatever wrong he had done. And anyone who stumbled across them would do a smart about-turn and march away, ignoring what they had seen, at least they would if they had even half an ounce of sense Tom, though, felt devoid of sense right then. He stepped forward.

"What's all this about, then, lads?"

Tall Man swiveled his head towards him. "Mind your own fuckin' business."

31

"I see," said Tom, stooping to put his bags down carefully, flexing his fingers as he straightened. "And what if I decide I want to make it my business?"

At that, Tall Man looked briefly at his two companions, nodded, and pushed himself upright. He took a couple of paces towards Tom, a menacing look on his face. *Keep going*, Tom urged him silently. *Keep going. Then we'll see how you cope with someone a little better at looking after himself than a kid.*

"Last chance," said Tall Man, now just a yard or two away, both skinny hands curled into fists. "Turn around and fuck right off or I'll make you fuckin' sorry."

"Is that so?" said Tom. And, before the other had time to respond, he had put his weight on his left foot and kicked out with the right. One second Tall Man was standing there, looking all threatening and aggressive. The next he was on the ground, writhing about and gasping for air, clutching at his groin which Tom's boot had turned in to a solid mass of sickening pain. Another well-aimed kick, this one to the side of Tall Man's head, and he went still.

The other two men exchanged glances, simultaneously shocked and angry, then relinquished their hold on the boy to turn their attention to Long Tom. The first of them, a shaven-haired thug with a dragon tattoo on his neck and studs in his nose and ears, lunged forward, swinging his fist wildly. Tom sidestepped the punch and delivered a jab to Tattooed Man's stomach. Air whooshed from his mouth. As he began to buckle, Tom's knee connected with his downturned face. Tom felt the man's nose break, saw blood splatter on the ground before the inert body of his opponent concealed it. By now the third man had obviously decided he would endeavour to succeed where his two friends had failed. This one, a rat-faced fellow with slicked-back hair, hurled a punch with such force that, had it been on target, would have ended the whole affair there and then. Tom, though, had seen it coming and dropped to his haunches. The miss spun Rat Face off balance. Tom finished gravity's work for it, straightening and placing a boot on his assailant's rump before propelling him face-first into the brick wall. The man joined his companions in blessed unconsciousness on the ground.

Tom paused long enough to interlace his fingers and lever his hands against each other, feeling the joints give a satisfying click. Then he walked swiftly up the lane to where the boy was lying motionless. He did not look good. Not good at all. There was a gash across his forehead maybe four inches long, and his face was a mask of blood. The skin around his eyes was puffy and bruises were already starting to emerge. Tom crouched over him, pressing his fingers to the boy's neck, feeling for a pulse and finding one, albeit one rather too weak to be considered healthy. Now what the hell was he supposed to do? He could leave the boy there, knowing someone would find him before long. No. That wasn't good enough. Having saved the lad from further punishment, it did not feel right to abandon him now. Tom tutted and cursed his own bad luck, but he knew what he had to do, and had to do quickly before the Three Stooges woke up. He clasped the boy's hands in his and hauled him over his shoulder, standing up with a grunt of effort and adjusting his burden until he had the lad in a passable fireman's lift. Staggering slightly, he made his way back up the lane, using one hand to steady the boy and the other to clasp the handles of the carrier bags which he was damned certain he would not be leaving behind. That done, he entered the narrow passage in the wall, which had not been there a second ago and which would cease to be there again the very moment they were safely through.

-FIVE-

Kelvin sat in the cold entrance area of the police station, a building that appeared to have changed little since it was built, probably a hundred years or more earlier. The floor, though, a tiled mosaic with a strangely Masonic emblem, was beginning to show signs of deterioration. He felt he had spent so much time here since Jessica went missing that he could trace every point of the emblem, complete with missing pieces.

Time had turned full circle. He felt as lost and frightened as he had six months ago when, with a feeling of sick dread growing in his stomach, he had raced here after being telephoned at the office by the police. Mary had already been taken into one of the interview rooms, but he remembered hearing her agonised cries long before he saw her. She had been uncontrollably distraught at first, but that had slowly given way to silence and a vacant look which Kelvin had found more unnerving than the hysteria.

The loss of Jessica had, effectively, signalled the end of their marriage. Not that they had exactly been living in wedded bliss, not for a good few years. They had been arguing more or less constantly, half the time not even knowing what the rows were about. Kelvin guessed the person who was right for you when you married them was not necessarily going to be right for you forever. People changed. He was not the same man he had been when they walked down the aisle, and Mary sure as hell was not the same woman. The arrival of their daughter had kind of brought them together, or at least stopped them falling apart, and they'd been fine for a while. But then Jessica had been taken and they were right back to where they were before.

35

The Ragchild

The station's outer door swung open and a tall man in a grey suit walked in. He looked somehow familiar, but that meant nothing. Over a thousand people could walk into the bank on any given day. The man pressed the button at the enquiry desk, then leant on the counter.

"Been waiting long?" he said to Kelvin.

"No. They're fetching someone for me."

The enquiry window opened and a middle-aged woman acknowledged the man with the briefest of nods. "I've been told to bring my documents in," the man said, handing over a clear plastic wallet. The woman removed the contents, two printed sheets of paper, then handed the wallet back.

"Insurance," she said, scanning the sheets. "Driving licence. Right. I'll take these through. You might as well have a seat."

And with that she slid the window closed and was gone.

"All this bloody fuss just for doing fifty-five in a fifty stretch," the man said, looking at Kelvin as if seeking his support. Kelvin was not taken in. People always said they were travelling slower than they actually were. He had been guilty of it himself. The man had probably been doing closer to sixty-five.

"You'd think maybe they might have something better to do."

"Sorry?" Kelvin said, not really listening to what the other was saying.

"No wonder the bloody crime rate is so high. They should be out there catching real criminals instead of hassling people who just slip over the speed limit."

Kelvin felt he ought to say something, but he did not know what. Neither did he particularly care. He had too many worries of his own to sympathise with anyone else. He could not help but feel the threads of his life were unravelling. First Jessica. Then Mary having what was probably close to a nervous breakdown. Then there was Tanya. Getting close to her was dangerous, but he could not help himself. He needed someone. Needed warmth and affection, someone he could just sit down and talk to. And so he found himself drawn to a girl who was too understanding and too beautiful for him to resist.

Tanya was a friend, he tried telling himself. That was all. He had not let it go any further than that, though Christ alone knew there were times when he wanted to. He had even fantasised about making love to her, with a vividness that had given him a painfully full erection. Stick to fantasy, he told himself. Fantasies don't hurt people.

He was snapped back to the present world by the electronic click of the security door opening. A familiar face appeared.

"Kelvin. Would you come through, please?"

Kelvin remembered him instantly: Detective Sergeant Bob Miles, the officer who had interviewed Mary when Jessica had been snatched. He was a big man, with a nose too crooked not to have been broken at some time, and cropped dark hair turning grey. He looked more like a criminal than a copper, but appearances were deceiving in his case. His manner was gentle and, Kelvin knew from experience, he was capable of great compassion. Right then, however, he looked deeply troubled.

Kelvin followed him through the security door and down a drably painted corridor. "You said Mary was here," he said. "Is she all right?"

Miles stopped and turned to face him, then made a so-so gesture with his hand. "She seems to be okay. The doctor took a look at

37

her a little while ago. Gave her a mild sedative and it seems to have calmed her down. Anyway, I thought it would be better to speak to you before the matter is taken any further."

"Matter? What matter?"

"Your wife was involved in ... in an incident a couple of hours ago." Miles looked almost embarrassed. "Luckily, I was on duty."

He continued walking down the corridor, Kelvin right behind him.

"What do you mean, an incident? For God's sake, what happened?"

"She tried to steal a baby."

Kelvin was stunned into silence. Steal a baby. Christ, what was going on? There it was again, that inexorable feeling that his life was falling apart. He could almost hear the stitches tearing as he tried to take in the detective's words.

"She thought it was Jessica."

Kelvin could not suppress the sudden wave of optimism which swept through him, just as it had many times in previous months. There was always a chance, he thought, always a chance, however remote, that Jessica could still be found. "Was it?"

Miles shook his head. "The baby was only six months old."

"The same as Jessica was when she was taken."

"That's right. Surely your wife understands Jessica would have been older."

"Is older, you mean."

"Sorry. Of course."

Kelvin rubbed a hand across his jaw, then shook his head. "To be honest, I don't know what Mary understands and doesn't understand any more. It's like getting Jessica back is her only reason for living. That's why she ... we ... can't give up hope of finding her. If we don't have hope we don't have anything."

"I understand," Miles said softly. "I've got kids of my own, and if anything ever happened to them I'd — well, I don't know what the hell I'd do. Maybe it would be best if you just took Mary home and tried talking to her later, away from here."

"Take her home? You mean ..."

"The parents have decided not to press charges. I explained about your wife and they remembered reading about Jessica in the paper."

"I don't know what to say. Except thanks."

"There's just one thing," said Miles. He seemed to be fumbling about for the right words. "They made it clear they felt sorry for Mary, but at the same time they did not think it would be, well, safe to have her wandering the streets like that."

"But what can I do about it? She was fine when I left this morning."

"Nobody's blaming you. And nobody is suggesting you should lock Mary in the house while you're at work. But the doctor thinks you should seriously consider getting help for Mary. Psychiatric help. I agree with him. So do that baby's parents. In fact they've made it a sort-of condition of not pressing charges."

"Don't think it hasn't occurred to me," Kelvin said, flinching as he remembered Mary's violent reaction when he had last broached the subject. "Where do I start?"

"The doctor rang the hospital and arranged an appointment for Mary to have a chat with one of their psychiatrists. She'll be in good hands, I promise."

He held out a piece of paper. Kelvin took it off him and looked at it. A name, a date, a time. Meaningless pencil scratches on cheap white notepaper.

"Please, make sure she goes," Miles said. "Your wife got off lightly this time, and so did that child. The next time it could be a lot more serious."

He stopped and opened one of the doors leading off the corridor, then stood to one side and gestured to Kelvin to enter. Mary was sitting at a table, looking incredibly small and defeated and bearing very little resemblance to the woman he remembered. When he called her name she did not move, did not even blink. It was only when he touched her arm and told her it was okay, they could leave, that she looked up at him, but her eyes no longer showed any real signs of life.

-SIX-

Sometimes he dreamed. Other times he lived in a state so close to a dream that there was virtually nothing between them. Captain, they called him, but he could never remember why. Probably the beard. Fucking thing stank and was alive with fleas and Christ knows what else, but it was there, a part of him, and that was that. All Captain sought was oblivion. And so he drank. He'd get through a half-dozen or so flagons of cider a day, at least during the first couple of days after he'd cashed his Giro. But when that ran out he'd find the money some other way. Beg it, steal it, threaten people for it as a last resort. He vaguely remembered the kid in the car park up near the train station earlier that morning. Easy pickings, even if the kid had been a lying little shit. Captain had put him straight on that, oh yes he had. Nobody ever lied to Captain.

Now he had a Tesco bag full of bottles of cider and two of whisky to boot. Not to mention a couple of tenners left over for tomorrow. Pity that stuffy-looking prick in the subway hadn't dished out some cash when he had demanded it. That would have seen him through, but oh no, that eerie freak in the long fucking coat had gone and stuck his nose in. Captain had heard some weird shit about him and had not survived on the streets for so long by fucking around with people he knew not to mess with. One day, though. Oh yes, one day.

Captain groaned and lay back on the stack of flattened cardboard boxes which served him as a bed. He had made a nice little nest for himself inside the hollow concrete base of a footbridge which stretched over Oystermouth Road. There was a small opening in one side, for maintenance he guessed. At night he would wedge some

41

cardboard up against it to stop dogs coming in and pissing over him. Okay, so the place may not quite be the fucking Ritz, but with a gallon or two of cider inside him topped up with a bottle of Scotch, he was hardly going to care.

It was early afternoon and hot. No, not hot. It was *fucking* hot, the kind of heat which made it hard to breathe and even harder to think straight. Thinking straight was not one of his strengths, but that was beside the point. Being inside a concrete box made the heat worse, but Captain was buggered if he was going to share his good fortune with that scrounging shit Verdon. The man was quick enough to bum fags or booze off Captain whenever he was short, which was often, but not so quick to pay him back. Hadn't tried to help Captain threaten the suit in the subway, not even after Captain had given him one of the flagons paid for by the car park kid's money. So when Verdon went off somewhere for a piss, Captain had a bolted for his hidey-hole with his one-way ticket to oblivion.

He twisted off the top of the first flagon and drank deeply. Bliss, he thought, smacking his lips with appreciation before drinking deeply again. Maybe five minutes later the bottle was empty, so he tried some of the whisky, just for a change. Not really the weather for Scotch, this, but it had been a long time since he had been able to afford anything better than the bottom-barrel brands, so what the fuck. Another flagon. More whisky. After an hour he could feel it start to happen. Captain and the world sort of went their separate ways. He could still sense reality but from a distance. The sound of the traffic lost its stridency, became as soporific as the heat. He had reached that hazy border between the worlds of consciousness and sleep, and hovered there while he fumbled with a bottle he could no longer see and could only just feel.

Captain had no idea why he sought oblivion in such a single-minded way. At times, like now, visions would worm their way into his mind. Lightning-fast glimpses of a burnt-out building, images of a woman and a child, the woman stunningly beautiful, the child a boy, dark-haired and handsome. When they appeared, unbidden, these visions were always accompanied by a feeling of gut-wrenching sadness. Strangers, but maybe they had been real, once, and close to him. Or maybe they had never existed, and were just phantoms conjured by drink. Perhaps he drank either to forget the past or to banish these ghosts from his head, but wondering too much about it made his brain hurt. Which was why, when the emptiness took him, he so gladly embraced it.

He slept a haunted sleep, waking to darkness and the certain knowledge that he was no longer alone. He tried to sit up, but found his sweat-soaked body had sunk deep into the mound of cardboard which had wrapped itself around him and now held him firm. Cursing under his breath, Captain tried to lever himself free. No good. He was as weak as a newborn baby from too much booze and too little food. "Oh, fuck it," he muttered and gave up his struggle, sinking back even deeper into the sodden cardboard. Then, louder, "Whoever you are, just piss off and leave me alone."

There was movement at the opening and Captain could see the silhouette of a head, backlit by streetlamps. It was only a fleeting glimpse, but it was enough to tell him the intruder was a kid. He felt himself relax. He could handle a kid, no problem. Hadn't he proved that earlier? For a moment he wondered if it was the little bastard in the car park come looking for revenge, but even in his befuddled state he realised how unlikely that was. Probably just some snot-nosed runaway fuckwit trying to find a place to stay out of trouble for the night. If so, he was out of luck. Captain did not take lodgers.

"You deaf or what? I told you to piss off."

"I have been looking for you," a small voice said.

Before Captain could respond he heard a sudden loud rasping sound, followed by a flare of light which made him screw up his eyes in pain. Through his closed lids he could see the flare subside into a softer glow. He opened his eyes again, blinking away tears, and saw a small boy sitting by the opening, holding a candle in one pudgy fist. The child's face seemed familiar, not unlike that of the boy in Captain's visions, only a few years older. He was maybe seven or eight. Hard to tell. And from a pretty rough background, to look at him. No clothes as such, merely rags. The bright, orange-tinged skin on the boy's face began to ripple and flow as he smiled a slow, angelic smile, but that could only be an illusion caused by the candle-light. Either that, or Captain had drunk one flagon too many that day and was hallucinating again.

"Who are you?" he asked.

"You know who I am."

"Listen, kid, I've never seen you before in my life. Understand?"

The boy raised an eyebrow, an adult gesture which looked oddly out of place on his cherubic face. "Come now. Of course you do. You remember the little boy you see every now and then? In your visions? When you dream of him, you dream of me."

Captain had not been born a bright man, and years of drink had wiped out too big a part of his brain, so these words brought only confusion. Yeah, it was possible. In his infrequent moments of lucidity he would sometimes wonder if the child in his visions was his son, long forgotten for whatever reason, and whether he was alive or dead. If he was still alive, assuming he'd existed in the first place, then maybe, just maybe, he might have gone to look for his father. Yeah, sure it was possible, but he sensed that was not what the child had meant.

"Are you ... are you my son?" he asked, already knowing the answer.

"No. Only what you dream about. Only what you seek. Oblivion."

"How the fuck do you know about that?" Captain demanded, suddenly angry. It was his secret. Oblivion. An unrelenting desire for nothingness, for a painless end to everything bad in his life. He knew he had not spoken of it to another living soul.

"I will give you what you want," said the child.

And for Captain the world ended. He was no longer inside his hot and lonely concrete home. He was no longer even Captain. He was lost in raptures of pleasure, adrift on an endless sea of soft warm light with no memories of the past, no cares or worries, living only for the eternally wonderous now. Oblivion was not heaven, he thought. It was so much better than that. And then came agony as consciosness rushed in and Captain was back in his old world, gasping for breath and crying like a baby.

"Please," he gasped. "Please send me back."

"I will," said the boy. "Later. First I need something from you."

And Captain, so hungry for oblivion, was happy to do whatever was asked of him.

-SEVEN-

Martyn had only ever been drunk once, at a school disco a couple of summers ago when a friend of his had taunted him into it. The following day, head pounding and so wretchedly ill that he swore he would never touch alcohol again in his life, he had found he could only recall occasional details of the rest of that evening. It was almost as if chunks of his memories had been stolen at random.

He felt like that now, only a million times worse.

It could have been day or it could have been night. Martyn had no way of knowing. For some reason his eyes would not open. Every beat of his heart sent an echo of pain coursing through his skull, which hurt so much he felt like someone had been using it for soccer practice. The rest of his body, or at least those parts of it he could actually feel, hurt almost as bad. Elsewhere there was numbness. That worried him more than the pain, until the dawning realisation that he had no idea where he was eclipsed all other concerns. Martyn lifted a hand, intending to wipe away whatever it was that glued his eyes shut, but the movement was accompanied by a bolt of agony so fierce that he whimpered, dropped his arm and lay perfectly still. He made himself breathe slowly and deeply, fighting back the sense of panic which threatened to take hold of him, conscious of the fact that he could only deal with this situation by looking at it calmly rather than by allowing fear to overwhelm him.

Okay, he thought. Okay. First things first. He was indoors. That much was obvious from the stillness and slightly musty smell of the air. And he was lying on something soft, a mattress, rather than hard concrete or damp grass. A hospital, maybe, except it was too quiet for that. He desperately wanted — needed — to know what had happened but, as on the night of the disco, he could recall virtually nothing. At the back of his mind were a few vague and jumbled images which may have been memories or the fragments of a dream. He seemed to remember wandering the city streets. Then he saw three men, shouting at him. And then nothing.

A door snicked open to his left.

Could be help, or more trouble. Martyn hedged his bets and kept still. Though still blind, he could smell, faintly, the acrid tang of cigarette smoke.

A man's voice, deep, lowered. "How's he doing?"

"Not bad, considering the beating he took."

The answer came from a woman, her voice soft and lilting.

Hey, don't talk about me as if I'm not here, Martyn said. Or at least tried to say. His throat, though, had seized shut and his mouth felt puffy and as dry as old paper. Again he tried to raise his hand. Once more the pain defeated him.

"I think I saw him move."

"Muscle spasms. Tom, I told you it will be a while before he wakes. I can do so much but his body needs time to mend itself. We shouldn't disturb him."

"Of course. We'll let the boy sleep."

With that, the door clicked shut and Martyn was alone with the silence. This time, when despair reasserted itself, he almost succumbed. Then something the woman had said, something about him having taken a beating, triggered an image. A single image to begin with, but followed swiftly by a second. That in turn triggered a third, which set off a whole domino cascade of memories, bringing the whole sorry story back to him with dizzying speed. The man in the car park, the drunk with the beard who had stolen nearly all his money. Later, staggering through the busy streets, aware of people staring at him but avoiding their gazes. Counting out the few coins in his pocket until he was sure he had enough to buy a coffee and donut from the McDonald's. Taking it into the lane behind to avoid more stares from the people in the restaurant. Then three men, the three thugs who told him to get the fuck away from their patch, blocked his way. One of them, tall and skinny, stepped forward and punched Martyn in the stomach. And that was it. All he remembered. And if the pain he felt now was anything to go by, that was probably for the best.

He still had no idea where he was, but for now that did not seem quite as important as it had. Maybe he was in hospital, maybe not. The main thing was that those people expected him to get better, even if it took a while, so it wasn't as if he was going to be crippled for life or anything. The two of them, that doctor and nurse or whatever they were, wanted to help him. They were looking after him, and that mattered. After his mother died, nobody, none of his relatives, not even his own father, had been interested in looking after him. Martyn never got over that, the feeling that everyone in the world neither wanted him nor cared for him. He had no idea what he had done wrong but it hurt almost as bad as losing Mum.

He didn't want to think about her, not now, not with his eyes so tightly closed that there would be nowhere for the tears to escape. But he couldn't help it. Thinking about Mum was the only thing that had kept him going every night when his father had come back from the pub, drunk and looking for any stupid excuse to give Martyn a hard time, which usually meant a beating. Between what he earned in the steelworks and the money the insurance company had paid out, Martyn's dad could afford to get smashed out of his skull most nights. The only good thing was that he got so drunk he could not possibly have remembered how much money he'd blown. Which made it easy for Martyn to steal the odd few quid here and there. It had been the only way he could get anything for himself, and even then he had been careful to keep whatever he had bought well hidden from his father's eyes. He wouldn't have been able to provide the explanation which would have been demanded of him. His life had been reduced to little more than fear or boredom at home and equal boredom, if not fear, at school. And the only reason his father had wanted him in school was because, as Dad put it, he could do without the fucking welfare people on his back. In the first few horrible weeks after Mum's death, Martyn had imagined her watching over him, keeping him safe. Before long he had known she wasn't. Either that, or she was doing it badly.

It had reached the point where he knew his father was just one careless blow away from killing him. So one morning he had taken Dad's wallet and a few keepsakes, and walked out of the house for what he knew would be the very last time. He could never go back. Even after everything bad that had happened to him since, he was absolutely sure he would never go home again.

He tried to imagine his luck had changed from bad to good. Okay, so a man had hurt him and stolen nearly all his money and then three others had kicked the crap out of him. But that was just the latest in a whole series of beatings, even if it was the worst. He could live with it. He was alive, wasn't he? Someone had found him, made sure he was taken care of. Maybe this was where it started to get better. Martyn began to relax, suddenly realising how desperately tired he was. There were no distractions, other than his thoughts, to keep him awake. All he could hear was his own rasping breath. Otherwise nothing disturbed the silence of the room, which struck him as a little odd. Surely he should be able to hear something, cars, barking dogs, anything. Then again, maybe it was the middle of the night.

Sleep soon overtook him. When he woke the pain seemed to have lessened. Even before he opened his eyes — and it took a few moments for him to realise, with no small relief, that he actually *could* open them — he could tell it was broad daylight. He blinked furiously, trying to clear his blurred vision, becoming aware as he did so that he was being watched. A girl stood at his side. She had long dark hair, and held what looked like a cloth. Her hand had jerked away from him as he came to. He tried to speak but his throat was still agonisingly dry. The girl turned briefly away, reached for something out of Martyn's sight, then bent over him, holding a glass to his lips. "Drink this," she said, and he did, gulping it down. It was only water, but it felt like liquid fire as it passed over his parched lips, burning its way to his stomach. He choked, coughing harshly, and the girl took the glass away. "Too fast," she said. "You haven't drunk anything for days. Take it slow, or you'll make yourself sick."

Martyn nodded and she brought the glass back to him. This time he was careful to take short, slow sips. Better. Much better. The water no longer burned. In fact, it tasted unbelievably sweet.

"Thanks," he said, in a voice so scratchy he hardly recognised it as his own.

"You're welcome," the girl answered.

"Where ... where am I?" he asked.

"Safe. That's all you need to know for now. Get some rest."

"But —"

"But nothing. Sleep now. We'll talk again later."

Martyn, feeling a burning need for company, almost called after her as she left the room, but thought better of it. The girl was right. He needed to sleep. He felt better for the water and his body did not hurt anywhere near as badly as it had the previous night, or whenever it was that he had first found himself here, but he was still desperately tired.

When he next opened his eyes the light had faded and there were shadows around him. Martyn felt good, almost incredibly so under the circumstances. He yawned before cautiously stretching his arms, braced for an onslaught of agony. Nothing. It was as if the aches and pains he had felt earlier were no more than phantoms, the remnants of an unpleasant dream.

Slowly, convinced his recovery was a short-lived deception, he pushed back the thin sheet that covered him, swung his legs off the bed and sat up. No problem, other than a little dizziness, but even that soon passed. Confident he really was okay after all, Martyn stood, but he was suddenly mortified when he realised he was stark naked. His embarrassment, which seemed stupid given that he was alone in the room, was rapidly superseded by shock as he saw the bruises which covered him, black and purple and yellow, clearly visible even in the dwindling light. His legs almost buckled, and he reached for the edge of the bed to steady himself, waiting for his heartbeat to subside before daring to move again. Once his chest began to feel a little less like it was on the verge of exploding, Martyn wrapped the sheet around himself and shuffled over towards the door, which for some reason he guessed would be locked. He tried the handle and was surprised when it turned easily in his grip. Pushing the door open a crack, relieved that no squeal of hinges announced his presence, he peered into the darkness beyond. There was a corridor, doors running the length of each side. Martyn strained to listen but he could hear nothing. No television, no radio, no voices. Weird. It was possible the girl and the man had gone out for some reason, but would they have left him alone in their house? He could have been a thief for all they knew.

"Hello there."

The voice so startled Martyn that he dropped the sheet, grabbed at it, fumbled it with fingers which through a combination of shock and shame at his nudity had turned to jelly, watched helplessly as it drifted in slow motion to the floor. As he stumbled back into the room the door was pulled open by a tall man who stood in the corridor, regarding him with a look that was somewhere between concern and amusement. The man reached down for the sheet and tossed it at Martyn, who pulled it around his shoulders and clutched the two ends together at his midriff. He was trembling, his mouth dry as dust and his skin prickly cold. When the stranger raised his right hand, Martyn flinched, remembering the beatings at home which as often as not began with that very same gesture, a prelude to the first slap. But the man did not strike him. He was, Martyn could now see, merely making a placatory gesture.

"Gave you a bit of a fright, did I, lad?"

Martyn nodded, not trusting himself enough to speak.

"Sorry. I was just on my way in to see how you were doing when you opened the door." The tall man nodded towards the back of the room. "Better if you stay in bed for now. I can tell from the fact that you're up and about that you're obviously feeling better, but you don't want to do too much too quickly."

"Okay," Martyn said, hoping the man had missed the tremble in his voice. He sat upright on the bed, back pressed against the wall behind, rearranging the sheet to cover himself, mind in a whirl all the while. Martyn just could not figure out what on earth was going on. Maybe the man and the woman had brought him home with them, but he could not imagine anyone doing that for a kid they'd found beaten up on the street, not these days. Unless, of course, they were a pair of perverts intending to kill him, a prospect he quickly forced from his mind. Could be a cheap hotel, he supposed, or one of those hostels that homeless people stayed in. He considered it best to say nothing, to ask no questions but to wait and hope the man would volunteer some information. Until Martyn had a clearer picture of his situation there was not a great deal he could do about it.

He was surprised at his own calmness. It was as if this were happening to someone else and Martyn was only experiencing it second-hand. Then again, he'd been through so much bad shit recently, maybe he was starting to get used to it.

The thought must have brought a smile to his face because the tall man, who had waited in silence while Martyn climbed on to the bed, suddenly spoke up. "Glad to see you looking better. You went as white as a ghost a few moments ago."

"That's because you scared me half to death."

"Ah, well, wouldn't want that to happen. I'm Tom by the way."

He held out his hand. Martyn hesitated, then grasped it. "I'm Martyn."

"Martyn it is. I guess you must be wondering where you are."

53

"There was a girl in here earlier. I asked her, but she —"

"She insisted you needed more rest first," Tom finished, nodding. "And she was right. You were in a mess when I brought you here, laddie. Fortunately for you, Rhiannon has what you might call a magic touch with people who've been hurt."

"She's a nurse?"

Tom laughed. "No, nothing as ordinary as that."

"So are you going to tell me where I am?"

"Sure. You're in Rhiannon's place."

"You don't live here?"

"Me?" Tom said, a look of genuine surprise on his face.

"Yes. I sort of assumed you two were ... you know, married or something."

"No, lad. Rhiannon's just a friend. A very good friend, mind you, but no more than that. I have my own place, a flat just like this, but the next floor down. The only reason I brought you here was because I knew you needed Rhiannon's help."

"Was I badly hurt?" Martyn asked, already certain of the answer from the memory of the horrendous pain he had been in when he first woke.

"Like I said, a mess. Deep gash on your forehead. Blood all over your face. A couple of broken ribs. Oh, and some really nasty bruises just about everywhere else."

Martyn sat in silence a moment, trying to take this in. The bruises were still there, but when he touched his forehead he could feel nothing, no trace of a scar, not even a scab. His ribs felt fine, too. Either the man was exaggerating, or Martyn had been out of it for some considerable time.

"How long have I been here?"

"Four days, give or take."

"What?"

"Four days. You took quite a beating. Rhiannon can work wonders, but even so all she does is hurry nature along."

Four days! That meant he had been away from home for almost a week. He wondered if his father was the least bit worried by now, whether he had called the police. More likely he had done nothing, glad that Martyn was out of his sight once and for all. It was then that Martyn realised he didn't much care if his father was worried or not. Right now he had too many other things on his mind. Like coming to grips with the fact that he had lost four days from his life and had no idea what he was going to do next. Sooner or later he would have to leave this place. He was not afraid of Tom now. There was something about his manner that effortlessly inspired trust. But while Martyn no longer had any doubts that Tom and the girl had only been trying to help, he was equally certain they would not want him there forever. Neither would he want to stay.

He looked up at Tom, who was idly staring around the room. "If I've been here four days, like you said, why aren't I hungry? I should be starving by now."

"People don't feel hungry here, lad. They don't feel cold, they don't feel hot, they don't feel anything. You won't be thirsty, either, now that your body has regained the fluids it lost. What you have to understand is ..." He trailed off, shaking his head. "It's not easy to explain, Martyn. Not easy to grasp, either. Best perhaps if we wait until you're well enough to go outside. It'll be easier to show you than to tell you."

"Come on, then. Let's go now. I'm feeling fine."

"You're not going anywhere," Rhiannon said.

They looked at the doorway where she was standing with folded arms, almost daring Martyn to attempt to get past her. He realised that, while he had heard her speak, he had not once laid eyes on her face. He wondered what she looked like. Young or old? Hard to tell from her voice, which was still as soft and musical as he recalled but firmer now, edged with steel. "What if I want to leave?" he said. "Will you make me stay?"

"Not at all," Rhiannon answered. "And I will not waste my strength coming after you to pick you up when you collapse. Which you will, believe me."

"I told you, I feel fine!"

"Of course you do," she said. "You feel that way now. Start walking any distance before your body's ready for it, though, and then tell me exactly how fine you feel."

Tom winked at Martyn. "I always find it's best to do as you're told, lad, when Rhiannon is in this kind of mood. Besides, she knows what she's talking about. If it wasn't for her, you'd still be pretty much dead to the world right now."

"You don't half talk a load of nonsense at times, Long Tom," Rhiannon said. "And it would hardly be fair for me to take all the credit. You saved the boy in the first place."

"Now you're making me blush."

"Hey, wait a minute," said Martyn, who could barely recall the thrashing he had taken, let alone what happened afterwards. He looked beyond Tom to Rhiannon. "Are you saying Tom stopped those men who were beating me up?"

"What do you think?" she said. "They weren't going to stop on their own."

Tom looked distinctly uncomfortable. "I talked them out of it."

"Of course you did," said Rhiannon, laughing gently. "For a man who relies on his wits to talk himself out of trouble, you have a pretty good right hook."

"Now that's not true. I have an excellent right hook."

Martyn's problems seemed to fade into the background as he listened to their easy banter. He sighed.

"Feeling tired?" asked Tom.

"Not really."

"You need more rest, all the same," Rhiannon told him. "Apart from anything else, it's getting too dark to go wandering around outside. Wait until morning."

Martin was about to protest but, as reluctant as he was to give in, he had to accept that Rhiannon was right. "Okay," he said. "First thing in the morning."

"Then that's settled," said Tom. "Oh, and by the way, you don't have to worry about strolling the streets in your birthday suit. Rhiannon has washed all your clothes and mended them. They're airing as we speak."

"What about my bag?" Martyn almost cursed himself for forgetting it.

"Don't worry," said Tom. "It's under the bed."

Martyn reached down and felt around until he touched the rucksack's familiar rough material. "Thanks," he said. "And thanks, Rhiannon. For looking after me and everything."

"Don't mention it," she said. "Now try to get some sleep."

She walked out of the room, Tom getting up from the mattress and following her a moment or so later. As he reached the door the tall man hesitated and turned back to Martyn. "I know nothing about you except your name, laddie, but it seems to me you've taken more than just the one kicking of late. Am I right?"

Martyn shrugged. "Sort of."

"Thought as much. Don't worry. You're safe, nothing can harm you here."

"You keep talking about here. But where is here?"

"In the morning," Tom said. "I promise. Good night, lad."

"Yeah," Martyn said cheerlessly. "Good night."

Once Tom had gone, Martyn slid down on the bed and stared at the ceiling, tugging the sheet over him though he did not feel cold. The gloom of the room was a perfect match for his mood. Strange how the streetlights hadn't come on yet. Maybe there was a power cut. Not that he cared. His mind was in too much of a turmoil to care about anything. Thoughts whirled crazily, out of control. Sleep, they'd told him. As if he could, what with everything he had to worry about. He closed his eyes, concentrating on trying to slow down his thoughts long enough to put them into some kind of sensible order, and within minutes he had fallen into a deep and dreamless sleep.

-EIGHT-

The little home Alice had made for herself by the river was the one place in the world where she felt safe. There was no one to protect her out on the streets. No one to save her from the sneers and the lewd comments which made her cheeks burn with shame and embarrassment. A woman alone was an easy target, but over the years Alice had learned to roll with the punches. Now she made sure she stuck to the places where there were plenty of people about, and was home long before it was dark, long before she could draw the attention of all those filthy drunks, the ones with liquid courage in their veins. Being raped once had been bad enough. She did not want it to happen again.

Traffic rumbled across the Tawe Bridge above her head, drowning out the soft lapping of the water which was her lullaby most nights. Getting on a bit now, she thought as as she shifted on the grubby old mattress which had been her bed for as long as she could remember. Arthritis made her bones ache so badly these days that she knew she would only survive the winter by finding a place in one of the hostels which dotted the city. Not that Alice was sure she wanted their help, not unless it came down to a straight choice between living and dying.

Come to that, dying might not be so bad. What, after all, did she have to lose? No home, no family, no life to speak of. Nobody would miss her when she went. There would be a pauper's funeral with no mourners present, just a priest to say some hollow words about a lost soul he neither knew nor cared about, and a few strong men to carry her coffin to a grave that would remain untended, becoming swiftly overgrown. Of course, Alice would be beyond caring then, so she tried to make herself not care about it now.

59

Oh, but that was hard. Because, while she had virtually nothing else, she still had her memories. Still remembered the man she had worshipped, the man she thought she would marry until the day he had looked her in the eye and said there was someone else, someone he loved more than he could ever love Alice. He had broken her heart, torn it apart in a way Alice had not imagined possible, and it had never properly healed. Maybe she could have fallen for someone else, eventually, had it not been for the pills and, later, her breakdown. Funny how she could remember most of her life before then, but hardly anything afterwards. A few dim, fragmented and hellish images of her time in the sanatorium were imprinted on her mind, but she had no recollection of her release or her first months alone in the city.

Still she mourned for the love she had lost forever, and the hope that had been extinguished with it. Alice accepted, but nevertheless hated, the fact that she would die with no one to hold her. That was all she wanted. A man, a kind man to embrace her in her final moments in this world. Had it not been for her strict Methodist upbringing and the abhorrence of alcohol that had instilled in her, she would have sought comfort in a bottle many years ago. Instead she relied on her dreams to get her through each day.

And then, whether by coincidence or by a miracle, she heard footsteps crunch softly on the gravel path. As a rule, this would be the signal for her to curl up and drag her torn and filthy blankets over her face, in the child-like belief that her inability to see anyone approaching somehow rendered her invisible to them. Not this evening, though. Alice felt calm. An inexplicable but powerful sense of well-being carried her up and took her away to some other place, where the prospect of abuse, whether verbal or physical, simply did not exist. There was no danger. None at all.

A man strolled along the path towards the bridge, holding the hand of the child who walked perfectly in step alongside him. Alice squinted until her eyes were little more than slits, but her myopia and the dying light left her unable to discern their features. Eventually they were close enough for her to make out a little boy and a man surely too old to be his father. When they reached Alice's home beneath the bridge they stopped, and the child looked at her, a half-smile on his face. He was dressed in clothes so tattered they resembled little more than rags. His companion, too, looked down on his luck. Filthy trousers, creased jacket, beard matted with dirt. Street people like herself, maybe, though that did not make them any less of a threat.

"Hello," the child said.

Alice said nothing in return. Instinct, the overwhelming need to draw as little attention to herself as possible, had taken over from the feeling of euphoria which had held her only moments before. Besides, it had been so many years since she had talked to another living soul that she suspected the power of speech was probably beyond her. She gripped the blanket tightly, ready to burrow underneath it if the child or his grandfather, or whatever the older man was, took a step towards her.

The little boy cocked his head to one side as though studying her. It was a curiously adult gesture. "I know you," he said. "Your name is Alice."

She should have run away then, sensing something was wrong, but the child's words so shocked her she was unable to move. Nobody knew Alice's name save Alice herself, and sometimes, on her bad days, even she had trouble remembering it.

61

"How how d'you know me?" she gasped.

The child shrugged. "I know everyone in this city. Is that not so, Captain?"

Until that moment the older man had stood at the child's side, as still as a well-trained dog commanded to heel. Now a flicker of emotion crossed his face, and he nodded once before his features slackened again. There was something about him that unnerved Alice. He did not seem quite all there. "Is that your father?" she asked.

"The child is father of the man," the boy replied with a sly smile. "But enough of this, my dear friend Alice. We have business to discuss, you and I."

"Business? What are you talking about?"

"Your dreams. I know what they are. And I can make them come true."

Alice shook her head in denial and confusion. The words seemed wrong, spilling as they did from the lips of a child. It was an effort to make sense of the world at the best of times, but what was happening now was far beyond her comprehension. Her dreams? Who on earth could know anything about her dreams other than Alice herself? Ridiculous. And yet the boy did not appear to be mocking her. Quite the opposite. He seemed deadly serious. Maybe the old man, Captain or whatever his name was, had put him up to it. Well, if he had, if this was some kind of cruel joke, then that old man was going to be sorry.

"You should go," she said. "It's time you were in bed."

"Oh, I never sleep, Alice. I cannot dream, you see. Which is why I try to help make other people's dreams come true for them whenever I possibly can."

Alice felt her cheeks flush with anger. "This is stupid talk, little boy. If that senile old sod with you thinks making fun of an old woman is funny."

"It is neither stupid nor funny," the child said firmly, silencing her. "You dream about a man. You dream that he never left you, that you never were forced to live on the streets. When you sleep you dream of yourself in a nice house with your devoted husband and your beautiful, loving children. Is that not what you see?"

And, for one brief moment, Alice not only saw it but actually lived it. Her life was exchanged for another long enough for her to experience what her world would have been like had she not been forced to follow the path that she had. When it was over, when the sounds of the river and the traffic returned, she almost wept with grief at the thought of what she had lost. "Please," she whispered. "Give it back to me."

"That is all you have ever wanted," said the child, his voice little more than a whisper. "Love, and a man to take you in his arms and keep you safe."

"Yes," Alice said hoarsely. "All I ever wanted."

"You can have it back. I ask only one thing in return."

Her vision was blurred and watery so she did not see Captain approach, becoming aware of his presence only when he put his hands on her shoulders and lowered his head to hers. Alice's lips parted with a soft wet sound at the touch of his tongue. It tasted of rot and dust and, as it slipped into her mouth, it suddenly began to pulse and grow, pushing downwards, filling the back of her throat. Alice gagged and started struggling, but then Captain's strong arms were around her, holding her tight, protecting her, and she relaxed, lost in a kiss

63

The Ragchild

which she prayed would never end.

-NINE-

The sound of sobbing seeped through the bedroom wall like penetrating damp. Kelvin reached out with one hand, his fingertips touching the textured wallpaper. He knew he should go to her, but no amount of comforting would make her feel any better. Nor would it assuage his own guilt at the way he was tempted to find solace in someone else's arms. Instead he lay motionless in the single bed in the spare room and listened to his wife cry, just as he had so many times before.

The alarm clock showed 5.30 in glowing red digits. Kelvin was tempted to cover his head with the pillow to block out the crying but it was hardly worth trying to get back to sleep. Instead he decided to get up and make them both a drink.

"Brought you a cuppa," he whispered ten minutes later, pushing open the door to her bedroom. He felt like an intruder as he waited for a response.

"Thanks," she said. "You didn't have to."

"That's why I did it," he said, putting her mug down on the bedside cabinet.

"Tea and sympathy," Mary said, sipping the scalding drink. Kelvin thought he detected a hint of her old self somewhere in the laugh she suppressed.

"No," he said. "Not sympathy. We don't need that. We just need to start facing up to things, that's all. We need to support each other".

"Support?" she said, voice suddenly harsh. "Is that what you call this?" She hurled the mug across the room. It crashed against the door, leaving a Rorschach stain on the white gloss. "When you say start facing up to things, you really mean forget about Jessica, don't you? That's what you really want. Try to pretend that it never happened, like she never existed. That way you can stop feeling guilty."

Kelvin felt his face redden. "What the hell do I have to feel guilty about?"

"You'd rather sit in front of the bloody television than look for your daughter."

"Oh, for Christ's sake, Mary. You know damned well I've looked for her. I drove miles, day after day, night after night, just praying I would see her. But I can't keep looking forever. And, besides, the police."

"The police!" she spat. "What the hell do they know? They are as bad as you. They want to forget about it too. But I'm not going to let them."

"I can't talk to you," he said, knowing that whatever he did now would be wrong. He moved to the door again, picking up the mug which had miraculously remained unbroken. "Not when you're like this."

"Walk away, why don't you. That's your way of dealing with everything."

Her anger dissipated as quickly as it had erupted and she turned away. It frightened him, the way her mood swung so abruptly between extremes. She needed help. Kelvin had promised Miles she would get it. Now he was not sure he could convince her to go, was not entirely convinced he should try. Maybe he did walk away from everything. If she had treated him like this a few months ago he would have had to choke back tears of anger or pain or frustration. Now he felt immune to it.

Mary had not emerged from the bedroom by the time Kelvin had showered and dressed. He pressed an ear to the door but could hear nothing. At least she was sleeping, he thought. Perhaps that would help. He went downstairs quietly. The row with Mary had killed his appetite, so breakfast consisted of just a second cup of tea. Kelvin drank it, barely registering the taste, then left the house, using his key to close the lock silently. Better to let Mary rest.

Kelvin stood beside his Escort, fumbling with the keys, accidentally scratching the paintwork near the lock. "Shit," he hissed, wanting to kick the car to vent some of his pent-up aggression. It was going to be one of those days when everything that could go wrong would go wrong. He finally managed to unlock the door and threw his briefcase onto the back seat in a temper. Glancing up at the house he thought he saw the curtain twitch. Maybe Mary was awake after all. He shrugged and slid into the car. If she would rather feign sleep than talk to him, so be it. Her choice.

Checking his mirror as he backed the car down the drive, he saw two figures leaning against the wall of the house opposite. They were watching him, of that he was certain. Were they waiting for him to clear off so they could break in, believing his house to be empty? He looked again and realised that one of them was a woman, the other a boy. Nothing to worry about, he thought, and drove off.

Mary looked out of the bedroom window from behind the curtains as Kelvin pulled away from the drive. Peace at last. A chance to think without his constant noise. Even the sound of his breathing was starting to annoy her. What hurt more was that he didn't even seem to be aware of his blatant lack of concern about Jessica.

Then she saw the woman and the boy across the road. The woman held something clutched to her breast. Something precious. She glanced up and caught sight of Mary looking at her, then turned her back to shield the bundle from view. A sound cut across the distant thrum of car engines. The sound of a baby crying. Her baby! The boy looked up at her and smiled, and he and the woman walked away.

"Wait!" Mary cried, running for the stairs. By the time she was stumbling through the front door with one arm inside the sleeve of her coat over her pyjamas, they were out of sight. No matter. She would find them. They had headed away from the main road, towards the end of the cul-de-sac. They had to have been going the wrong way, she thought. Perhaps they would be coming back any minute and she would meet them. But as the end of the road came into sight there was nobody about save an old man putting out black rubbish bags ready for the dustmen.

"Where did they go?" she asked.

"Sorry?"

Mary was aware of the curious look he gave her, dressed the way she was, but chose to ignore it. "The woman with the baby. And the boy."

"Didn't notice any baby. But a woman and a boy went down the lane a couple of minutes ago. They can't have gone too far. You should be able to catch them."

Mary darted away without a word. Of course he would not have seen the baby, not the way the woman had held it tight to her chest. But there was no doubt in her mind that it was the same woman and boy. Catching up with them was all that mattered. The lane led across farmland which had not yet been sold to housing developers. As she reached the top of the track she caught sight of two figures in the distance, emerging onto the road at the far side. With the slope of the hill in her favour she started to walk faster until she was jogging, then running, heart pounding, in an attempt to close the distance between them. At the gate she had to stop to catch her breath. Her spirits sank as she saw the woman drive away in an old camper van.

"Bloody gypsies!" a man said from the other side of the hedge. Mary jumped. She hadn't noticed him standing there, waiting while a dog joined to his hand by a lead relieved itself. The man was shaking his head angrily.

"Sorry?"

"Gypsies. A load of them set up camp at Morfa. Buggers have been nosing around here a couple of days now. Trying to find something to pinch, no doubt."

"Morfa?"

"Yeah. Near to the stadium."

"How long have they been there?"

"Too bloody long, if you ask me. Got no time for scroungers like them."

"Right," Mary said and started back up the lane. She could catch a bus from the end of the estate and be there within half an hour. Of course she would have to call at the house first. Not just to get dressed; she had left without any money.

"You all right, love?" the man called after her.

"Yes," she said. And she was, now that she knew where her baby was.

-TEN-

It was light when he woke. Martyn lay on the bed, sheet crumpled on the floor where it had fallen sometime during the night, staring in astonishment at the bruises which had faded to the point where they could barely be seen. Impossible! They had been so deep, so vivid, it should have taken days, weeks maybe, for them to heal. Definitely more than just a few hours. Yet there was the proof. Right before his eyes.

There was something weird going on here. The absolute silence, the lack of street lighting, his own unnaturally fast recovery ... it was all wrong, out of kilter with reality, or at least the reality he was used to. Perhaps that was why Tom and Rhiannon were reluctant to tell him where he was. They were holding back, that was for sure. Well, if they were not prepared to talk to him, he'd find out for himself. If he was lucky, if Tom had gone back to his own place and Rhiannon was asleep, he could be out and away before they even knew he was gone. He knew he ought to thank them for looking after him, but curiosity prevailed over gratitude. Time for answers.

His clothes lay neatly folded at the foot of the bed. Martyn blushed when he saw them, realising they must have been brought in while he slept. Hopefully it had been Tom who had brought them in. His cheeks burned as he imagined Rhiannon seeing him asleep, nude, the sheet no longer covering him. But it was too late to worry about that now, he thought as he dressed. As soon as he was fully clothed he reached under the bed for his rucksack, then slid his arms through the straps and adjusted them until the rucksack was held firmly against his back. After a final quick glance around the room to make sure he had left nothing behind, he padded to the door and opened it as quietly as he could. This time there was no voice to startle him. A stained and faded red carpet ran the length of the corridor. Good; it would muffle the sound of his footsteps. At the farthest end was a door which he assumed was the way out of the flat. Martyn felt nervous and had no idea why. It was not as if he was running away from trouble. If anything, he felt bad about leaving without saying goodbye. Despite that, however, his palms were slick and his heart thumped madly in his chest.

No point in hanging around, he thought, and began to walk along the corridor, praying there would be no creaking floorboards beneath his feet to give him away. In the end it was Martyn's own sense of decency, rather than the floorboards, which proved decisive. One of the doors to his left was wide open and, through it, he could see Rhiannon. She stood at the window, silhouetted by the early morning light, her back towards him. Keep going, he urged himself. She hasn't seen you. But he found he could not move, could not leave now without saying something to her. In the same way that Tom had seen the suffering behind the physical pain in Martyn, so Martyn could sense there was something troubling Rhiannon. Nothing he could put his finger on, but he knew it was there. Maybe it was simply down to like recognising like.

"You can leave if you want," she said, without turning round.

Martyn felt too guilty for words.

"But I know Tom will be disappointed," she continued. "He promised he'd explain everything. I'll say this for Tom. He always keeps his word."

"I'll wait for him," Martyn said, half-hoping Rhiannon would believe that was what he had intended all along. He stepped into the room and Rhiannon turned to face him so that he saw her, really saw her, for the first time. It should have been her eyes that first caught his attention, so startlingly blue were they. Instead he could only stare at the taut, dry skin which covered her forehead and part of her right cheek, criss-crossed with tiny scars and made all the more painfully vivid by the contrast with the smooth milky whiteness of the flesh which surrounded it. She raised a hand to briefly touch the damaged skin, and Martyn immediately looked down, ashamed.

"I didn't mean to ... you know ... stare."

"Don't worry. I've become used to it over the years."

Martyn could tell she was just trying to be kind. No way you would get used to something like that. It was so unfair, especially as Rhiannon was the most striking woman he had ever seen. Even with the scars she was beautiful. He wondered what had happened, and almost died when he heard himself ask the question aloud.

"A fire," she said, eyes far away.

"Sorry."

Rhiannon's gaze met his directly. "And what about you, Martyn? What could happen to a boy your age to make him want to run away from home?"

"How do you know I was running away?"

She shrugged. "Call it a guess."

"Okay. You're right. My mother died. My father beat me a lot. That's it."

"Life can be tough, Martyn, but we can be, too. You'll survive, don't worry."

Loud heavy footsteps from outside silenced them. As they

neared, Martyn heard whistling, interspersed with snatches of a song sung in a loud and deep voice.

"That'll be Tom," Rhiannon said, the ghost of a smile on her face. "Right on time. Not that time has much to do with anything around this place."

Here we go again, Martyn thought, groaning inwardly. But he kept quiet, knowing what the answer would be if he asked the obvious question.

As promised, Tom did indeed explain everything, as best he could, although it sounded downright crazy. The first two of them clumped down the stairs from Rhiannon's flat in silence, nerves making Martyn feel slightly queasy. They followed one flight, then another, before leaving the building through a stout wooden door. Martyn jerked to a halt as they stepped outside. The early morning light was strong enough to dazzle him after he had been inside so long, but even so he could tell at a glance that the street was absolutely empty. It hit him straight away. No people, no cars. He looked up at the sky. No birds, either. He should have been able to hear traffic and trains, voices, birdsong, anything, yet there was nothing. He shivered. This was the first time in his life he had experienced total silence, and he did not like it one bit. It was as if some supernatural force had spirited away every living thing save Tom and Martyn himself.

"It's quiet around here," he said, thinking this was the understatement of the year.

"Always is," Tom said. "You get used to it after a while."

The tall man pulled a pack of cigarettes from his pocket, took one out and lit it with a match which he ignited with his thumbnail.

Martyn pulled a face, hoping Tom had not noticed, and turned away from his companion. He was conscious for the first time of the purity of the air. Its sweetness made the sulphurous, faintly sickly odour of the match, coupled with the cigarette smoke, all the more overpowering.

"They're no good for you," he said.

Tom blew out a long stream of smoke. "Huh. You sound just like Rhiannon. Always telling me I should give them up, that smoking will kill me in the end."

"She's right."

"No, she's not," Tom said, with an affectionate smile. "And she knows it. But the thing is, she's a healer and I suppose it's hard for someone like Rhiannon to shrug off the idea that smoking is bad. Truth is, nothing can harm you round here, lad. Not these things at any rate. Come on. Let's take a walk and I'll tell you what's what."

Without another word he set off. Martyn hesitated for a moment or two then followed him, feeling the sun warm the back of his neck as he walked. His leg muscles felt cramped and aching to begin with but they soon loosened up. Either that, or he was too distracted to notice the pain. The houses that lined the street were three-storey and grand, but empty-looking, their sweeping bay windows masked with thick layers of grime and bereft of curtains, nets or blinds. Looking around, Martyn could not see a single satellite dish, nor any aerials perched on the roofs. The buildings appeared old, yet simultaneously new. Martyn had the uncomfortable feeling that if he opened a door he would see nothing behind it except timber props and the expanse of a studio lot. The weeds growing up through cracks in the road and pavements only served to reinforce that impression. Everything looked wrong, like elements of a scene that should be viewed in black and white, not colour.

Tom turned left and Martyn scurried after him, not wanting to be left alone in this strange place. There were no houses now, just a long row of shops which looked every inch as deserted as the houses and equally out of date. He saw old-fashioned canopies. Below them, signs advertising outfitters, tobacconists, ironmongers and a barbers. There were others, such as a haberdashery and milliner, whose function would remain a mystery to him. The shop fronts looked different to any Martyn had seen before, in that they were made entirely of wood rather than metal or plastic.

One of the largest buildings proudly announced itself to be Swansea's Finest Department Store, yet if the contents of the display windows were anything to go by, it sold nothing but shadows and dust. Maybe today was Sunday, Martyn thought, which would explain the silence and emptiness. Not that he believed it for a minute. It felt more like the end of the world.

They reached a break in the row of shops and Tom led him through a creaking wooden gate into a park. Well-kept grass rustled softly beneath Martyn's feet, a welcome change from the monotonous hollow thud of his boots on concrete. Ahead was an ornate bandstand and, in a circle around it, a handful of benches. Tom sat down on the nearest, leant back and stretched his legs out in front of him. He closed his eyes and raised his face to the sun, looking entirely relaxed. It was only when Martyn had settled down beside him that he opened his eyes again. He reached into his pocket for his cigarettes, pulled them out, hesitated and, to Martyn's relief, put them away again. "I told you it takes a little getting used to," he said.

"I don't understand," Martyn said. "The place is so quiet. Where are all the people? And why aren't there any cars around?" He bit his lip and fell silent, knowing that if he carried on he would start to sound even more scared than he felt.

"There's nothing to be afraid of."

"Who said I was afraid?"

"I can tell these things, just like I can tell you don't like me smoking." Tom gave him a wink and a quick smile, then his face grew serious. "None of this is easy to explain, Martyn. God knows I had a hard enough job getting used to it myself, and I was nearly three times your age when I first came here."

"So where are we? Where is here?" Martyn demanded.

"Okay. Tell me, do you know what the word 'sentient' means?"

Martyn shook his head.

"All right," said Tom. "If something is sentient, it is aware. Aware of itself, and of others. That's the first thing you'll have to accept, Martyn, if any of this is going to make sense to you. I don't know how exactly, or when, though I have my theories, but somewhere along the line the place you call Swansea became sentient."

"Are you trying to tell me," Martyn said slowly, "that this place is alive?"

"Not exactly alive, lad, no. But it *is* aware."

"That's a load of crap," Martyn said hotly, furious with Tom. After everything he had been through, all the pain and confusion, the last thing he needed was some smart-arsed old man winding him up. He stood, and would have stormed out of the park had Tom not grabbed his rucksack and pulled him back down on the bench.

"It's the truth, lad. Or at least it's the truth the way I see it."

"Come off it, Tom. Cities don't live! They're just bricks and cement and stuff."

"And people. Don't forget them, Martyn, because I think they're the key."

Martyn rubbed his face with both hands. "What are you talking about?"

"Tell you what," Tom said. "Let me tell this my own way, no interruptions. I'll tell you everything I know, as well as the bits I don't know but think I've figured out. Hopefully by the end of it, you'll believe me. If not, talk to Rhiannon about it. And if you don't believe her ... well, we'll cross that bridge when we come to it."

"Why don't I just go and ask her now?"

"Rhiannon isn't a great talker, lad. Besides, I promised you I'd give you an explanation, and that's what I'm going to do. So. Do we have a deal?"

Martyn shrugged. He had nothing to lose, he supposed. "Yeah, okay."

"Good." Tom stared into space a moment or two, as if collecting his thoughts. "Swansea wasn't always a big city, as you probably know," he said. "Wasn't always a city, either, come to that. Used to be just an ordinary town until the Sixties. Anyway, it grew. And it just kept on growing, thousands more people coming here every year. Think of all that energy, Martyn, all that power, that vitality. See what I'm getting at?"

"You're saying we made the place come to life?"

"More or less, yes. Imagine the city is a body, the streets its veins, and us, us incredibly energetic humans, we're the blood coursing through those veins."

"Okay, I follow that. I'm not saying I believe you, mind. And you still haven't explained what all that has to do with this place being so quiet."

"One thing at a time," said Tom. "Don't forget, I told you the city was sentient. I didn't say it was alive. That's your interpretation. It's not as if I've been able to sit down and have a good long chat with it. What I'm telling you is either what I've figured out for myself or what some of the others around here have told me."

"Others?" said Martyn. "But I haven't seen anyone apart from
—"

Tom raised a hand. "No interruptions, remember? Right, this is the part you're going to find the hardest to accept. There's no easy way of putting it, so I'll tell you straight. There are two Swanseas. The one you know, and this one. Try and picture two corridors, in a hotel maybe, separated by a wall. You can't see who or what is in the other corridor, and they can't see you. Got it?"

Martyn nodded.

"Good. Now imagine there are doors running down the length of the wall. Doesn't matter which side of it you're on, you can open one of the doors whenever you feel like and walk straight through to the other. But, and here's the thing, the doors are invisible to some people. Not everyone can see them, but you can."

He paused long enough to light a cigarette. Martyn said nothing.

"This is what I think happened," Tom continued, his words draped in smoke. "Swansea first became aware of itself before the war. The Second World War, that is, before you ask. Then came the bombing raids. The buildings were destroyed in the physical world, but I think Swansea, somehow, remembered them. It kept them alive in its memory until it was strong enough to rebuild them, and that's what it did. One of those two corridors is the world you know, Martyn. The other is here. Old Town."

"Old Town?"

"That's what we call it. Helps us separate the two."

Martyn tried to absorb everything Tom had told him, and failed. It was too far beyond his experience, his understanding of reality, to be able to comprehend. And yet he was here, wasn't he? In a city town, whatever, where the buildings were so old-fashioned they could have been plucked straight out of a history book. A tiny part of his mind still insisted he was the butt of a practical joke, but Martyn knew that could not possibly be the case. The proof was all around him.

"Anyway," Tom continued. "To my mind Old Town needs its own blood to stay alive. That's why it lets us in. Probably why it takes care of us while we're here."

"What do you mean, takes care of you?"

"We don't age here, Martyn. You could stay a hundred years and you'd still be a kid, exactly as you are now. It's give and take. Old Town needs us as much as we need it. We keep it alive, so it keeps us alive while we're here. When you're in Old Town you don't get hungry, you can't be ill. You don't get too hot and you don't get too cold. You must have noticed that."

Martyn hadn't. He did now. He could feel the heat of the sun but it was not in the least uncomfortable. And, while he had not eaten for the best part of five days, he was not at all hungry. Sure, he had been parched when he first awoke, but after he had drunk those few glasses of water he did not feel like drinking any more.

79

"Is that how I got better so quickly?" he asked. "Because of ... Old Town?"

"In a sense," said Tom. "But you can really thank Rhiannon for that. Her touch can cure all ills, given time. To be honest, I don't know whether Old Town works through her, or if it's her own special gift."

"Then why doesn't she do something about those scars on her face?"

"Never asked," Tom said. "Maybe she's worried she would lose the gift. Then again, maybe she just wants to keep them. A reminder of her old life. Most of us like to hang on to something, Martyn. You don't have to sleep here, but I know a lot of people who do. And you can eat if you want, though it doesn't matter if you don't. Me, I like to smoke, while a friend of mine drinks at least a bottle of whisky a day."

"It doesn't harm you at all?" Martyn asked, remembering Tom's earlier remark that the cigarettes would not hurt him.

"Not in the least. In fact, the only time we're likely to get into trouble of any kind is when we leave. Most folks refuse to set foot in Swansea, especially those who have been here longest. I suppose I'm the exception that proves the rule. I've been here for well over fifty years, but I love exploring the other place. I don't stay there long, mind, but I go there as often as I can. And if anything happens, not that it ever has, then Rhiannon will take care of me. Unless, of course, I get myself killed."

"So what would happen if you died in Old Town?"

"I told you, that can't happen."

"Never? Suppose somebody shot you or stabbed you. Would you die?"

Tom raised an eyebrow. "Good question. Can't say I've ever thought about it, or if I did it was so long ago I've forgotten. First of all, Martyn, the people here are all good folk who lost their way in the other world. The homeless, those without hope, the dispossessed. They love it here, wouldn't do anything to harm Old Town or each other."

He dropped the cigarette butt to the grass, stepped on it, then stood. "Best if we get back now. Give you a little time to get used to the place. I know it's an awful lot to take in, Martyn, but you will come to accept it. You have my word on that."

Martyn did not reply, convinced he could never get used to it.

He spent the rest of the day sprawled on the bed, staring at the ceiling and ignoring Tom's gentle attempts to draw him into a conversation. Eventually Tom stopped bothering him, and Martyn was left alone with his thoughts, not sure if he wanted to be but certain he was not in the mood for idle chat. Time and time again he went over what Tom had told him. It made sense, in a totally crazy kind of way, but was so far beyond his experience that he could not come to terms with it. Cities that rebuilt themselves after they had been destroyed! People who could smoke and drink and God knew what else, without it harming them. And time stopping still, somehow, so that nobody aged a day while they were here. What had Tom said? That Martyn could stay there a hundred years and still be a kid. The thought simultaneously intrigued and repelled him. Admittedly, it would be nice to live forever but the idea of being an ancient old man in a teenage kid's body was a pretty sick one.

He wrestled with his thoughts for hours, and at the end of it decided to leave.

The place was too weird. Simple as that. It was so creepy there was no way he would go outside on his own. And if he could not go outside, there was nothing for him to do but what he was doing now. Nothing, forever and ever. Thanks but no thanks, he thought. He liked Tom, even if he was a bit on the strange side. Then again, living here for half a century would do that to you, Martyn supposed. As for Rhiannon, he really wished he could have gotten to know her better. She struck him as kind, if shy, and even though he knew she would not want him to, he felt sorry for her. The sadness he saw in her eyes was like a reflection of his own despondency.

It didn't matter. None of it mattered. He could not stay.

They walked away from the house in silence, Martyn with his hands in his pockets, head bowed, avoiding Tom's gaze. Telling them he was leaving had been harder than he'd imagined it would be, but he managed to get the words out. Saying goodbye to Rhiannon was even tougher. He liked her, he really did, and when she told him she was sorry he was going but that she understood his reasons why, he almost changed his mind. But then it came back to him, that horrible image of himself looking the way he did now but incredibly old and almost insane after years of doing nothing.

He had no idea what he would do once he was out of Old Town. All he had to survive on was a pocketful of change. No matter. He'd manage somehow. He had to manage. If worse came to worst he'd go to the police station, tell them everything that had happened with his father. Surely they wouldn't send him back after hearing his story. Martyn would rather live in a foster home than return to the life he had left behind. Anything was better than that, even roughing it.

"This should do," Tom said, disturbing Martyn's reverie.

"Should do what?" The only thing Martyn could see was a narrow lane that separated two terraces of houses and emerged into a similar street.

"Look at me," said Tom, and Martyn did. "Now look back."

The lane was unchanged, except for the fact that it no longer led anywhere in Old Town. Martyn could see large green bins, the type kept round the back of shops, which he remembered seeing in the lane behind McDonald's just before he was attacked. Traffic sounds drifted towards them. A small voice in his head told him he should be shocked by this unnatural transformation, but he simply took it for granted. Maybe he was getting used to the place after all, despite his misgivings.

"Here," Tom said, holding out his hand. Martyn looked down and saw that his friend, which was how he now thought of Tom, held a folded wad of banknotes.

"I...I can't take that," he said.

"Of course you can. Plenty more where this came from."

"No, really," Martyn said. "I can manage."

"Take it." Tom reached out and placed the money in Martyn's hand, folding the boy's fingers around it. "Use it to stay out of trouble, if that's possible."

Martyn felt suddenly choked as he pushed the money into his jeans pocket. While he was still reluctant to accept, he also understood it would be stupid of him to refuse. One day, he swore, he would pay it back somehow. "Thanks," he said, wiping his eyes with the back of his hand. "For, you know, everything."

"Don't mention it," Tom said, smiling. "Tell you the truth, getting you out of that little mess you were in made a pleasant change.

83

I was getting bored."

"Will I see you again?"

"Sure you can, if that's what you want. Don't forget, you can always come back here. Now that Old Town knows who you are, the way is always open."

"Except I won't know how to find it."

"Don't worry about that. The way will find you. Just take yourself to some quiet place in the city, where nobody can see you." Tom looked quickly down the lane. "Speaking of which, you'd better get going, lad, before anyone notices."

"Okay," Martyn said. He wanted to say more, but the words wouldn't come.

"Go on," Tom said softly. "Be off with you."

So Martyn went, not daring to look round because he knew that, if he did, he would change his mind and go back, which would do him no good at all. He had to at least try to make something of his life in the world he was used to and, of course, he now had an option other than to turn himself in to the police should all else fail.

The lane which joined the two worlds had muffled the sound of the traffic. It deafened him as he stepped into Swansea. The air smelled dirty after the sweet purity of Old Town, and the sun was unbearably hot. But, despite all this, Martyn was glad he could experience such sensations once more. It made him feel ordinary again, whereas in Old Town he had been ... something else.

He turned to call goodbye to Tom, only to see that he would have been, quite literally, talking to the wall. The way had closed up behind him, though he had no doubt it would have opened again, had he wanted it to and had the coast been clear. For the first time in ages he felt good about himself. Martyn pulled the rucksack straps tight and began to walk into the city which he now considered his home.

-ELEVEN-

He had not slept, but it made no difference. He still felt as if he was caught up in the middle of a nightmare. Coming home to find the house empty, aware as he was of Mary's state of mind, had been bad enough. But when, three hours later, she had still not returned, had not even phoned to say where she was, he began to panic.

He'd rung the police, demanded to speak to Bob Miles, only to be told the detective was on the night shift. The receptionist promised she'd get Miles to return his call as soon as possible. To Kelvin's relief, he did so a little after nine-thirty, and had arrived at the house less than thirty minutes later.

The man's professionalism had not covered his concern, and his obvious humanity had almost reduced Kelvin to tears of gratitude. Miles had taken a recent photograph of Mary away with him, telling Kelvin to sit tight and wait.

Come the following day he was still waiting.

He had hardly slept, thinking about Mary, the baby, Tanya. All of it just going round and round in his head with none of it really making any sense. He had given up on the tossing and turning at around five-thirty, and from then until late morning had tried to catch up on some work. He'd read and re-read the pages of briefings but none of it had really sunken in. By lunchtime he'd no longer been able to keep his eyes open. Shortly afterwards he'd fallen asleep on the settee. When he woke it was after six. He realised with a pang of despair that Mary had been missing for over 24 hours. He decided to take a cold shower, hoping that would help clear his groggy senses.

The telephone, after remaining stubbornly silent all night, chose to ring within seconds of him stepping under the icy blast. Kelvin grabbed a towel while he was running, trailing it behind him as he took the stairs quickly, then clutched it to himself as he picked up the telephone in the hall. "Hello?" he managed between laboured breaths.

"It's Miles. Sorry I've taken so long to get back to you."

"Have you found her? Found Mary?"

"No, but she has been seen."

"Where?" Kelvin asked, heart pounding both from his sudden run down the stairs and a growing sense of excitement tinged with panic.

"We circulated her description, showed the photo, made a few enquiries. Buses, trains, taxis, the usual sort of thing. A bus driver said he was pretty sure that he dropped her off somewhere near Morfa. You know, the athletics stadium."

"When?"

"Yesterday, around lunchtime. He remembered her because she paid to go into the city but got off early. And because she was looking so flustered, as he put it."

"But I don't understand why she would be heading for Morfa."

"She could have been meeting someone," Miles said.

"Doubt it," said Kelvin. "Her family's from away, and she hasn't bothered with her friends at all since Jessica went missing."

"There is another possibility," Miles said. "A small group of travellers have set up camp near the stadium. A couple of our uniform boys paid a visit, had a look around. No sign of Mary, but a few people there remembered someone matching her description walking by a couple of hours earlier. You know. She may have gone back there later, if she was desperate enough for somewhere to spend the night."

"You haven't been there again to check?"

Miles sighed. "Sorry, Kelvin. I wish I could have, but we're a bit short this week. Besides, and don't take this the wrong way, the super won't thank me for spending time chasing a missing person who's only been missing a day."

"I understand," said Kelvin. "And I appreciate what you've done. But I'm going frantic with worry here. Would you mind if I went to the camp myself?"

He would have gone anyway, had only asked out of courtesy. Miles thought it over for a second. "Okay," he said finally. "Our boys reckon the travellers were peaceful enough. Just one thing. If you find Mary, no trying to force her to leave."

"But I can't leave her there! She needs medical help, you know that."

"That's besides the point. If you so much as touch her and she makes a complaint ... well, I'm sure you don't want to cause any more heartache for yourself. It might be an idea to take someone with you. One of Mary's friends. Even if she refuses to deal with you, she may talk to someone else. Assuming she's there."

"Right," Kelvin said. It made sense. "Thanks for the advice."

"One other thing."

"What?

"Let me know how you get on."

"Sure. As soon as I get back."

"Good luck," said Miles, then hung up.

Kelvin held the receiver to his ear long after the line had gone dead. He knew who to call, but first he had to think carefully about what he would say. There was nobody else he could turn to or would want to involve. Forced to admit that he had no other choice, he started to tap out her number.

"What's so important?" asked Tanya as she got into the Escort. She had been waiting around the corner from her parents' house, not wanting to be seen by them. Kelvin knew that they would not approve, and despite Tanya's bravado he suspected that deep down she really wanted to conform. When he had pulled into the street he had not recognised her, standing there in a short red leather skirt and black leather jacket. In another part of town she would not have been standing alone for long.

"I couldn't tell you on the phone."

"Why not?" she laughed. "Afraid it's being bugged?"

"If I'd told you, you might have said no." Might have? She definitely would have refused, he knew that, and he hated himself for the subterfuge.

"What do you mean?"

"It's Mary," he said. "She disappeared yesterday, but the police think they know where she is. I need someone to come with me."

"And you thought of me," she said, folding her arms across her chest. "You hardly speak to me for days, no matter how much I want to be with you, yet when bloody Mary is in trouble you call me!"

"I didn't know who else to turn to. Mary knows you."

"Yeah, she knows me. She doesn't know that her husband has been sneaking out to be with me, though, does she?"

"That's not fair," he said, aware that he probably deserved the dig.

"Fair! What's fair got to do with it? When have you treated me fairly?"

"Look, this isn't about you or me. It's about Mary."

"Isn't it always? She doesn't seem to want you anymore. She may need you, but she doesn't want you. Sometime you will just have to let her go."

"Maybe," he said. "But not before I'm sure she's safe."

Kelvin told her about Mary's disappearance while Tanya listened without comment. Her silence made him uncomfortable, made him doubt whether she would be of any help when the time came.

"So you don't even know for a fact that she's there?" she asked.

"She'll be there."

"What if she isn't? Or she is, but doesn't want to leave?"

"She will."

"How can you be so sure?"

"Tanya, she's looking for attention. That's all."

"And you're happy to go on giving it. Do you get a kick out of being the white knight all the time? Always turning up to rescue her whenever she's in trouble?"

"It's not like that," he said, knowing that it was. Then again, it was easy to be a hero when someone depended on you.

The rest of the journey passed in uncomfortable silence. Just before they reached Morfa, Kelvin pulled over to the side of the road. He flicked off the lights and killed the engine. Then he reached out to take Tanya's hand. "I'm sorry if I upset you. But try and imagine how I feel. Mary disappeared yesterday. Do you blame me, white knight or no white knight, for being worried?"

"No, I don't suppose I do," Tanya said, squeezing his hand.

Kelvin leaned forward and kissed her. It struck him, not for the first time, how much she was like Mary used to be, a long time ago. They both had blonde hair and athletic figures, but the similarity went beyond just looks. Sure, Tanya could be childish and demanding but, Christ, she could be wonderful, too. He loved the way she laughed, just as he used to love the way Mary laughed. But that had been before. He doubted he would ever hear his wife laugh again.

Reluctantly, he opened the car door. "Might as well go take a look. You stay here. I shouldn't be too long."

"I'd rather come with you," Tanya said, refusing to let go of his hand.

"And I'd rather you waited. I don't think there's likely to be any trouble, but you can always find a phone box and call for help if I don't come back."

The last had been said with a wink to show he was joking, but Tanya did not seem to find it amusing. "I don't like this," she said. "Please, Kelvin. Don't go."

"There's nothing to worry about," he said, extricating his hand from hers. He gave her one last smile of encouragement, and set off towards the stadium.

-TWELVE-

Some girls were training in Morfa Stadium. Captain had a clear view of them from where he sat, transfixed, on a boulder close to the riverbank. He found himself hypnotised by the pendulous swaying of their breasts as they jogged along the running track. What he wouldn't give for a little time with a pair of those pert little darlings, he thought, smirking as his penis unfurled into a satisfyingly rigid erection. Not that he was in a position to do much about *that*. The child had made Captain's obligations clear. Watch out for trouble. Keep off the drink. Do nothing to attract attention. As long as Captain obeyed, he was allowed glimpses of the oblivion he craved, tantalisingly brief but so ecstasy-inducing, so ecstatic that he would do nothing to jeopardise.

He tore his eyes away from the stadium and glanced across the adjoining field to where their camp had taken shape. Nearest to his vantage point was a shelter made from breeze-blocks, with sheets of corrugated iron for a roof. It had no windows and a single narrow opening at the front, across which a battered wooden door sat lopsided on its hinges. Beyond lay a motley collection of vans and campers and beaten-up old cars. Rising between them, like islands in a sea, were tents in which most of their recruits now lay sleeping, or doing whatever it was the child caused them to do when he did not require their services. Captain had seen them. They were like corpses.

A few people stumbled about the camp, carrying this, fetching that, all for some purpose way beyond Captain's comprehension. He had no idea how long it had been since the child had found him. Could have been days or weeks. Not much longer than that, he guessed, judging by the still-searing weather. His uncertainty had nothing to do with drink. For the first time in God alone knew how long, he was sober. No, it was down to the fact that each time he emerged, crying and trembling, from oblivion, he and the boy were in a different part of the city and there was someone else with them. The first had been that crazy old bitch living under the river bridge. And there had been plenty of others since after. A guy who'd been jailed for touching up kids. Some burn-out who'd lost his business and his family soon after. Three hard cases they'd found badly beaten and unconscious in a lane, who had staggered to their feet when the child appeared, for all the world like he was Christ raising the dead.

Oh aye, they'd gathered themselves a right little following. But it was nothing compared to what waited for them when they got to Morfa. Must have been a couple of hundred people or more, Captain guessed, all of them with blank eyes, stumbling around the place like fucking retards. What the hell the child wanted them for was anyone's guess, and Captain was not about to ask. Much as he hated to admit it, even to himself, Captain was afraid of the boy. Half the time he didn't even know where the kid was, but he felt him all the same, a constant presence in the back of his mind. There was something going on, some plan being hatched or falling into place, that much he knew from the times their minds were joined. Captain had the impression they were searching for something, though he didn't know what. There were pictures in his head. A place with old buildings. People, some familiar to him, like that weird bastard in the trench coat he'd seen in Swansea. Captain hoped *that* one figured in the plan. He had a score to settle with him, yes sir. Then there was the whining kid Captain had robbed in the car park, the one who had lied to him about the money. As for the rest, they were strangers as far as

93

he could tell; a young woman, another a few years older with dark hair and scars on her face, a well-dressed man. Whether they were anything to do with the child's plan or just memories thrown up from the hazy days before he turned sober, he had no idea. but he was in little doubt that all would be made clear before long. He just had to be patient.

And just as he would not consider questioning the boy, neither had he any intention of asking how someone so young could do everything this one had done. Why spoil it for himself? Captain had it easy, after all. No putting up tents, no humping shit about the place for him, no sir. It was as if the boy trusted Captain enough to make him his second in command, or something like that. The kid occasionally sent him into oblivion but otherwise left him alone and, for the last couple of days at least, had hardly spoken a word on those rare occasions when he could actually be seen around the place. Maybe he had other things on his mind. Could be that whatever all this was about, it was coming to a head. That was fine by Captain, who was bored shitless with sitting around doing nothing, without even a drink to help him pass the time.

Funny. He'd thought giving up the booze would be murder, but it had really been a piece of piss. Maybe the child had something to do with it. He could work some miracles, that one. Like setting up a camp this big, with so many people, without getting any grief from anybody. When Captain had been in the city the police had moved him on or banged him up so many times, it became as familiar as farting or picking his nose. Yet here, nothing. At the very least Captain had expected the council or whoever owned the land to turn up and order them off. There were roads running right alongside, but the camp did not attract even the most fleeting of glances from any passing driver that Captain had noticed. Then again, it could be that they just didn't see anything out of the ordinary. The child could do that. The child could do anything.

Scratching his balls and yawning widely, Captain turned back to face the stadium, but a flicker of motion in the periphery of his vision made him glance to the ground. A rat, filthy and scrawny, was rustling through the grass at his feet. It halted as if sensing it was being observed, head raised, nostrils twitching. Captain's hand shot forwards and down, grabbing the rat before it could move. It squealed and thrashed furiously, but Captain's grip was solid and he held it before his eyes, inspecting it closely. Dirty fucking things, rats, he thought, seeing the myriad tiny motions in its fur. Then again, his own beard was flea-ridden and rank, so maybe he was a good one to talk. The small body arched and twisted, as the rat tried to bite him, so he squeezed with more strength than he realised he possessed, and heard a crack. The rat went limp. It gave him a thrill, this sudden rush of power, this feeling of having as much control over the fate of the rat as the child had over him, so he tightened his grip further still and felt a hot wet bursting in his hand. He looked at the glistening mess which dripped from his fingers and stained the grass red, and he understood, really understood, for the first time that the child was not the only one who could do whatever he wanted.

Captain could, too. Just as long as he stayed with the boy.

Whatever I want, Captain thought, and raised his hand to his mouth.

-THIRTEEN-

Tom sat with his feet up on the park bench, folded coat serving as a pillow, and tried to concentrate on the book he was reading. It was a Louis L'Amour, one of his favorites, but for the past few minutes he had been merely scanning the same lines over and over, his mind elsewhere. Something about the boy had gotten to him. He had only known the kid a couple of days, but it seemed a hell of a lot longer than that. Which he found hard to understand, because Tom made a point of not getting too close to people. Life was easier that way. You couldn't hurt anyone, or be hurt by them, if you kept them at arm's length. Yet Tom had put himself at risk in the outside world to rescue the boy, and still felt bad that he had let him leave alone. Sure, the money would hopefully be of help, but it would not save the lad if he got himself into trouble again. Tom sighed and closed the book, not even bothering to make a mental note of what page he was on. There was no point. He couldn't remember a damn thing about the story.

He stood and pulled on his coat, dropping the paperback into one of its pockets, then started walking with no real idea of where he was going. For the first time in as long as he could remember, he felt restless. As a rule he was, if not exactly happy, then certainly content with his life in Old Town. Why shouldn't he be? Here he was provided with almost everything he could possibly need, immortality included. And if there was anything he wanted which was not to be found in Old Town, the place provided him with the wherewithal to buy it. Tom lacked nothing. He knew he should be satisfied. But, of late, everything no longer seemed to be enough. It was as if the kid had somehow opened a hole in his life, and Tom knew there would be no rest for him until he had managed to close it again.

He debated going back to the city and attempting to track the lad down, before dismissing the idea. Assuming he succeeded, what was he supposed to do then? Martyn had left because he wanted to leave, not because anyone had forced him to. He probably would not take kindly to Tom coming after him. Tom could understand that; he would not like anyone sticking their nose into *his* affairs, that was for sure. Besides, the boy knew how to get back into Old Town if and when he ever wanted to return. Trouble was, that was no help as far as Tom was concerned; he still felt ill at ease.

When he finally became aware of his surroundings, Tom was mildly surprised to discover he had walked straight back home. Not that home seemed quite the right word for it, given that he never ate or slept there.

He paused at the steps leading up to the front door, lit a cigarette and paced back and forth along the pavement while he smoked it. By now the reason for having returned had become obvious. Whenever he had something on his mind, a problem he needed to solve, it was always Rhiannon he turned to. She was the sole exception to his self-made rule about not getting close to anyone. Tom often wondered why that should be. Maybe it was the fact that she used her hands to heal, not hurt, without once asking for anything in return. There was a selfless quality about her that enchanted him, and an air of tragic mystery that aroused his sympathy. The funny thing was that, although she was loathe to speak about herself, Tom felt as if he knew her better than anyone else in the world.

He dropped the cigarette butt to the ground and stepped on it, fanning the air around his face with his hand. It would not make the slightest difference, as Rhiannon would still smell smoke on his clothes and breath and give him a mock-serious lecture, but he always went through the motions just the same. He opened the door and took the stairs up to Rhiannon's floor, calling her name as he entered the flat.

"In here," she said, though she need not have bothered. Tom knew where to find her. She liked to sit in the room at the front, its window overlooking Old Town's streets and, at this time of year, catching the best of the light. Through the glass Tom could see buildings which had long since disappeared in the outside world. He often thought about how he could stand in this exact same spot in the other Swansea and be in the middle of a shopping precinct surrounded by a mass of people rushing this way and that, as if the world was about to end. It never failed to send a shiver down his spine.

"I wondered how long it would take you," Rhiannon said, too busy with her needlework to spare a glance for Tom.

"What's that supposed to mean?" he asked, lowering himself into the chair opposite Rhiannon's and trying his best to sound nonchalant.

"It's the boy, isn't it. You've been on edge from the moment he left."

"You're imagining things," Tom said. "I hardly know him."

"Whatever." Rhiannon executed a few deft twists and turns with the needle, tied a knot too small for Tom to see, then used her teeth to snap the thread. She had been sewing buttons on to a blouse, which she now folded carefully and placed on the arm of her chair. "Deny it all you want, Tom, but I know you too well to buy the act."

Time to admit defeat, Tom thought. "Okay. You're right. Don't ask me why, but I get this nagging feeling of guilt about letting him go back there alone."

"It was his choice. He could have stayed here if he'd wanted to."

"I know," Tom said, wanting another cigarette. "I keep telling myself the same thing but, you know, it doesn't actually make me feel any better about it."

"He'll be fine. Martyn's strong inside, stronger than he looks."

"You're missing the point. What I want to know is, why the hell am I letting it worry me? Why should I care about him? Like I said, I hardly know the kid."

"Maybe you're getting soft in your old age."

Tom grunted, refusing to rise to the bait.

"Seriously," Rhiannon said, "you like to project this tough guy image but I can see straight through you. At heart you're a good man, Tom."

"Oh, cut it out."

"It's true,." Rhiannon said, giving him a smile which he could not stop himself from returning. "All of us need someone to care for, Tom. It's what makes us whole, makes us human. And none of us can tell exactly why we care for certain people. It's just the way things work out. Don't worry about it. You're no different to anyone else."

"I guess not," said Tom. "You know, crazy as it sounds, I considered going after him. But then I thought maybe he wouldn't appreciate that."

"He might do. Then again, you could be right. He might not. It's his life, Tom, and he's old enough to make his own decisions. Probably best if you leave him to it."

Tom nodded. Rhiannon was right. She always was. "And what

99

about you, my girl?" he asked. "Who do you care for? Who is it that makes you feel human?"

"Now that," she said with another of her dazzling smiles, "would be telling."

-FOURTEEN-

Free of pain and with money in his pocket, Martyn felt relaxed and ready to deal with anything life threw his way. At first he had been shocked when he counted the notes Tom had given him and found they amounted to almost a hundred pounds. It would be so easy to blow it to, buy anything he felt like. But Martyn was sensible enough to know he would have to manage the money carefully if he was going to succeed in surviving on his own. That meant finding not only food, but somewhere to sleep. The first of these was easy to deal with. Not long after leaving Old Town he felt a rumble in his stomach which, as the morning passed, developed into a persistent demand. The McDonald's was inviting, but a sandwich from the market was cheaper.

So far, so good. But he still had to figure out where to spend not just the next night, but every night after it. No way would he go back to the car park, and not just because of the beating he had received at the hands of that crazy old man. The place was too exposed. Okay to chance it once or twice, but any more than that and he'd be asking for trouble. Martyn chewed the problem over, along with his food, as he sat in Castle Gardens and, enjoyed the warmth of the sun on his face. Finding somewhere to stay. That was going to be a tough one, all right. A hotel was out of the question. Apart from the fact that it would eat up his money in next to no time, he would never be able to come up with a good enough story to explain why a kid who looked young enough to still be in school needed a room. Next thing he knew the police would be called and he'd be back to square one. Same went for a hostel. Martyn had no real idea how the places worked, but he very much doubted they'd take him in with no questions asked.

101

The Ragchild

It was a headache, and one that stayed with him as he wandered around the city before heading towards the beach for a change of scene. By mid-afternoon, his skin dusted in sand and feeling sore and hot where it had seen too much sun, his buoyant spirits were sagging. He simply could not come up with an answer. Okay, he could go back to Old Town if push came to shove, but he didn't want to do that. Not because he had any problem accepting the place. He had been there, seen it for himself, hadn't he? And while Tom's story about how it came to be took some swallowing, it made a crazy kind of sense if you thought about it long enough. Which he had. No, it had nothing to do with Old Town, Tom or Rhiannon. It had everything to do with Martyn. By going back he would be admitting he was incapable of making it alone. That in itself would be bad enough; the fact that he'd have given up within hours would make it so much worse.

As he walked back through the city he saw a dog, and for a moment his mind was cast into confusion. It was exactly like Jake, the old mongrel which had been a part of his family for as long as Martyn could recall, and his one source of regret when it came to leaving home. This dog was about the same size as Jake, with the same black, white patched fur and the same half-asleep eyes. It was tied to a leg of one of the fancy wrought iron refuse bins which dotted the pedestrianised centre, a frayed length of rope serving as a lead. The dog was sprawled out as if oblivious to the never-ending flow of people around it.

Martyn halted as he passed, bending down to ruffle the fur on the dog's head. "Who's a good boy," he said, not knowing if it was indeed a boy, and not caring, either. It was what he used to say to Jake, and the familiar words brought as much comfort to him as they obviously did to the dog, whose tail swiped the air at Martyn's touch.

"Don't worry," a girl said from behind. "He's soft as shit. Won't bite."

"Didn't think he would."

"Yeah, well, he likes you all right. Tail's gonna unscrew itself in a minute."

Martyn turned around. The girl, who looked a few years older than him, was dressed in denim jeans and a khaki tee shirt that was faded and torn but looked clean. Her hair was cropped and dyed a vivid pink. A procession of studs ran the length of each ear. There were rings in her eyebrows, and one in her lower lip. Wedged under one arm was a small bundle of *Big Issue* magazines. Homeless, then. Just like me, he thought, surprised at the ease with which he now accepted that previously unimaginable status.

"I'm Kate," she said. "And that soft mutt there is Sonny."

"Martyn," he said.

She smiled at him, revealing straight white teeth which, what with her studs and dyed hair, were not what Martyn would have expected. "And what's a young boy like yourself doing all alone in the big city, eh, Martyn? Lost, are we?"

"Just out for the day," he said, not sure why he lied but suspecting he would be better off the less he said about himself. "Catching the train back in a bit."

"Is that right," Kate said. While it was obvious she did not believe him, she did not push the matter, and Martyn relaxed. She was probably just being friendly.

"Hey," she said. "Look who's here."

The sun was in Martyn's eyes. He lifted a hand to shade them

103

and saw a man walking towards them, a large bottle of water in one hand and a small, battered metal bowl in the other. He set the bowl before Sonny and poured a generous amount of water which the dog immediately began to lap up.

"Who's this?" the man asked, voice sounding genial enough. "Found us another new recruit, have you, love?"

"This is Martyn. He took a right shine to Sonny here. The feeling was mutual."

"How're you doing, Martyn?" The man looked quite a bit older than the girl. Tall and thin, with long brownish hair and a goatee, and dressed much the same as Kate except his jeans were black and his tee shirt a soiled yellow. "I never tell anyone my real name," he said with a broad wink. "But you can call me Joe."

"How do you manage?" Martyn asked before he knew the question had formed in his mind. He immediately regretted having spoken. Then again, they might tell him something that could help him improve his own situation. "For money, I mean."

Joe shrugged. "You get by. Most of the time. There's places you can go, charities and stuff. And the *Big Issue*, of course. Don't get me wrong. There are times when you're so hungry or so cold and wet that you can hardly bring yourself to move. But most of the time you get by."

"We're hoping that's gonna change after today," Kate said.

"Why?" said Martyn. "What's happening?"

"Word is there's this big camp forming a couple of miles away." Kate reached out and clasped Joe's hand. "Some mates of ours headed out there last night."

"Guess the fact that they haven't come back means it must be okay," Joe said, pouring more water for the dog before swigging from the bottle himself.

"Where is it, this camp?" Martyn asked.

Kate raised an eyebrow and her lips formed into a knowing smile. "What's it to you? Thought you were catching the train home before long."

"Just wondering."

"Uh-huh. Thought so. It's by Morfa Stadium. Be nice to get out of this shitty city for a couple of days. You have no idea how it feels when you ask someone to spend a rotten quid on a magazine and they stare right past you like you're not even there. Least we won't get that in the camp. We'll be with our own kind."

She gave Martyn an appraising glance. "Travellers're always welcome in places like that, kid. Might be worth remembering. In case you miss your train."

"Thanks," Martyn said. "But I'll be all right."

He said goodbye and stepped into the fast-flowing stream of people, catching a last glimpse of Kate as she briefly raised a hand in farewell. The crowd swept him around the corner into Oxford Street and he lost sight of her. God, he had been so tempted to say yes, he would go to the camp with them. That was what Kate had obviously been hinting at. She was okay, and that Joe bloke had seemed so, too, in a laid-back kind of way, but two beatings in as many days had left him wary of strangers. Furthermore, while he stayed in the city he was part of, or at least still close to, the kind of life he was familiar with and understood. Besides, he knew where this camp of theirs was, and though he had never been to Morfa Stadium he doubted he would have much trouble finding it if things didn't work out.

The Ragchild

Less than two hours later he was in the Quadrant bus station, asking a woman in the enquiries kiosk which bus would take him to Morfa. He had given up. The money in his pocket meant food would not be a problem for quite a few days, as long as he was careful, but the problem of finding somewhere safe to sleep had defeated him.

The bus was full. Martyn sat on an inside seat, rucksack on his lap, while a woman burdened with shopping bags coughed and fidgeted next to him as they left the city behind. They passed the Parc Tawe shopping complex with its hangar-like buildings, crossed the river bridge and headed north along a twisting road. To Martyn's left the Tawe was a mass of tiny sunbursts, flowing so sluggishly it appeared drained by the afternoon heat.

The bus jerked to a halt with an asthmatic wheeze and the woman with the shopping bags got up unsteadily and tottered down the aisle, puffing with every step as if in sympathy with the brakes. Martyn was relieved she was getting off before he had to, having dreaded the prospect of trying to manoeuvre past her. He jerked forward as the bus pulled away, then closed his eyes and leant back in his seat, feeling suddenly tired. For one brief moment he felt himself teeter on the verge of sleep, so he forced his eyes open, worried that he might miss his stop.

Before long he could see a handful of floodlights rising above the industrial buildings which lined the riverbank. The bus bore left at a roundabout, crossing another bridge, and the rear of the main stadium hove into view. It was modern in style, all red brick and glass, with bisected cylindrical tubes running the length of its roof. But the entire place looked deserted, with no sign of any camp that he could see. Martyn began to wonder if Kate and Joe had got their facts wrong.

Maybe they had deliberately lied to him. For a laugh, perhaps. He didn't think so. They had seemed genuine enough. Still, he was here now. Might as well have a look around. Spotting a bus stop ahead, Martyn stood and walked down the aisle towards the driver. He leapt off the second the vehicle had jerked to a halt, and followed the road until he found a path leading down towards the stadium.

It was as he walked past a tyre depot that he first saw the camp. There was a mass of tents and vehicles in a field on the far side of the stadium, but the place looked just as deserted as the playing fields. Somehow he could not imagine this becoming his new home, even if only temporaily. He felt slightly nervous as he drew closer, but that feeling was miles better than the frustration and impending sense of panic which had started to grow in him as he wandered through the city. At least now he was trying to do something to improve his lot, rather than hanging around feeling sorry for himself.

The path gave way to a narrow road which terminated at the entrance to the field. Giant boulders blocked the way, leaving Martyn wondering how all those cars and vans had managed to get in. Even if someone had been able to roll them out of the way, why would they go to the trouble of moving them back again? There must be a second entrance to the field. He stopped as he reached the first of the boulders, trying to summon the courage to go further. Something did not feel right. He had built up a picture in his head: of plenty of people like Kate and Joe, sitting and listening to music or knocking back a few cans, talking, having a good laugh. But the scene before him was like an earthbound version of the Marie Celeste, in which everyone who had been there had been spirited away. All he could hear was the flap of canvas as the breeze picked up and, above that, the rumble of distant traffic and the cackling laughter of the seagulls which dipped and wheeled over the Tawe. Something sagged inside him. There was no way he would stay here. It was way just too creepy. Just as he was about to turn and retrace his steps to the bus stop, he caught a glimpse of movement within the camp. Martyn ducked behind the boulder, then slowly peered around it.

Three people walked towards him, two old women flanking a man and holding him by the arms. The man shouted something Martyn could not make out, and though he struggled he was no match for the women. That made Martyn think it must be some kind of game. Even he could have shaken off the two women, both of whom looked old enough to be his grandmother. He watched, intrigued, as they guided the man to a ramshackle building on the opposite side of the field from Martyn, maybe fifty or sixty yards away. It was made of breeze-blocks with a roof of corrugated iron. One of the women hauled the door open and they propelled the man inside with surprising force. Closing the door behind him, they turned their backs to it, then stood as still as machines whose power had abruptly been cut. Even from his vantage point he could see their eyes were wide and unblinking, and staring in his direction, almost as if they could see right through the boulder and knew he was hiding there.

If it was a game, Martyn thought, it was the weirdest game he'd ever seen.

Right now he wished he had never listened to Kate and Joe's talk about the camp. He desperately wanted to get out of there, to catch the bus back to Swansea, find his way into Old Town again. Which, he realised, was what he should have done in the first place. And would have done, had he not been so pig-headed about surviving on his own. It would not have been giving up, not if he thought of Old Town merely as somewhere safe to spend the night. Which is what he had wanted all along. Nobody said he could not leave when he wanted to. Leaving this place, though, was a problem. If he moved out from behind the boulder the two old women were bound to notice, and there was something about the absolutely rigid way they stood that made him shudder.

He sighed and sat on the ground, his rucksack pressing uncomfortably into his back as he leaned against the boulder. It felt like a punishment he deserved. Martyn glanced at his watch, swearing quietly when he saw it had just turned six-thirty; it would be at least another two hours before the light really started to fade. Which meant he had a very long wait, unless the two women moved off in the meantime or he managed to summon enough courage to make a dash for it. Right now that did not seem likely.

Maybe ten minutes passed before he heard voices, deep and gruff. Peering around the boulder again, he could see a group of people walking towards the breeze-block shelter. One of them, a woman, appeared injured and was being carried by two of the others like a roll of carpet. They walked past the two old woman standing sentry, heading for the river. Martyn felt sick when he saw who was leading the strange procession. It was the bearded old man who had attacked and robbed him the in the car park. Heart pounding, hands suddenly slick with sweat, Martyn pulled his head back and closed his eyes, hoping to God they were not coming his way and wondering what he had gotten himself into here. Seeing the bearded man had dashed any last hope he had harboured that perhaps the camp was all right after all.

Martyn heard footsteps crunch on gravel to his left, too close for comfort, and shuffled around the boulder as far as he dared without showing himself. Even then it was a near thing. If the bearded man and his companions had not their backs to him as they passed by, they would have spotted him for sure. Now Martyn could see the woman they carried was unconscious. Blonde hair cascaded around her face, but the breeze lifted it aside to reveal a necklace of vivid bruises encircling her throat. Worse, there was blood on her face, a lot of it, and Martyn suddenly knew with horrible certainty that she was not unconscious, but dead. He wanted to turn away, but he found himself hypnotised as they carried her to the edge of the riverbank. Then he heard a booming splash as her body was dumped into the Tawe.

It became hard to breathe and even harder to think. He had never been this afraid in his life. What frightened him most was the realisation that if the bearded man saw him, which he surely must when he turned away from the river, Martyn would probably suffer the same fate as that poor woman. He heard them moving towards him again and he squeezed his eyes shut, praying silently, pressing tight against the rock as if he were trying to force himself into a place of concealment inside it. His body tensed, anticipating a shout to ring out at any time, the signal that he had been seen. For once, though, luck was on his side. The group did not even glance his way. They merely strolled into the camp as if nothing untoward had happened, and vanished amid the cluster of tents.

For a minute Martyn could not move. Then the trembling started and, try as he might, he simply could not make it stop. He felt the urge to throw up and fought it, aware that the two old women were only a short distance away and would no doubt hear him retching. It took every ounce of willpower Martyn possessed, but eventually he managed to bring his rebellious body under control. He knew exactly what he had to do now. Sit still, make no sound, wait for it to get dark. Then he would run as fast as he could for the road, find a telephone box, call the police. After that he would walk or catch a bus back to Swansea and, from there, Old Town and safety. He loosened the straps of his rucksack and lowered it to the ground. Might as well get comfortable, he reasoned.

Maybe he would not have to wait as long as he feared, either. For all he knew the two old women would bugger off long before it got dark. They may have already left, not wanting to risk being spotted so soon after the body had gone into the river. Slowly, very slowly, Martyn looked around the edge of the boulder. Which was when he felt a hand grab him by the shoulder and a deep voice ordered: "Don't move."

-FIFTEEN-

Either Bob Miles was guilty of the understatement of the year, or the camp had grown enormously in a matter of hours. It was a haphazard maze of vans and cars, most of which Kelvin doubted were legally roadworthy. Packed around and between them were tents, some quite new, others worn and stained, and held together with patches, the rest little more than tarpaulins lashed to crooked makeshift frames. There must have been a hundred or more of them, but absolutely nothing, not the remains of a fire nor even a scrap of litter on the ground, to suggest that anyone lived there. It was like a graveyard. A canvas graveyard, where tents came to die. The thought brought a smile to his face, which quickly faltered when he realised it was all down to nerves.

Kelvin wandered at random through the camp, ready to bolt at the first sign of trouble, fighting the urge to give up and get the hell out of there. He could be back with Tanya in a matter of minutes. After all, what did he think he was doing? The police had checked the place out and said there was no sign of Mary. He had no reason to suspect they were wrong. And even if they were, if he somehow managed to track her down, Kelvin was not sure what he could do to persuade her to come home with him. Anyway, was there much point in trying? Their daughter was gone and would not be coming back. Kelvin hated to admit it but it was true. All he hoped was that she was not dead, that someone was taking care of her at least as well as he and Mary would have. And since Jessica had been the glue which had held them together, her absence meant their marriage was irretrievably over. He knew it, and accepted the fact that he would have to let his old life go. Not yet, though. He could not abandon Mary when her state of mind was so fragile. Maybe he still cared for her, a hangover from all the time they had spent together and the memory of earlier, happier days. Or was it down to the fact that he didn't want his conscience troubled should she do anything stupid?

"Aren't you the shit," he said aloud, suddenly filled with self-loathing, yet at the same time aware that he was wasting his time. Mary was not here. There was no reason for him to stay. Kelvin sighed, knowing he had deluded himself into thinking he could succeed where the police had failed. The only sensible course open to him now was to return to Tanya and let fate take its course. Maybe they would end up in bed together tonight, maybe not. Unless his mood improved, it was unlikely.

Turning to head back to the car, he noticed something half-buried in the grass to his right, shimmering as it reflected the sun. He dropped to one knee and reached down for it, his hand closing on warm metal. It was a locket, fashioned into the shape of a heart and instantly familiar, loaded with memories. Fingers trembling, Kelvin managed to prise it open, the two hinged halves folding back to reveal a tiny photograph of himself on the left side, another of Jessica on the right. He snapped it shut, curled his fist around it tightly, telling himself that finding it changed nothing. It only meant that Mary had been here at some point. But she was gone now, along with everyone else. The only unanswered question was whether she had dropped it accidentally or on purpose. If the latter was true, perhaps it meant that she too had finally come to terms with the fact that Jessica was gone forever, taking their marriage with her.

There was one other possibility, that the locket had been taken from her by force, a prospect he quickly discounted once he studied the chain closely and saw that it was intact, and its clasp undone, a sure sign that Mary had taken it off deliberately. Kelvin pushed the locket into his jeans pocket and stood, brushing grass off his knee.

Which was when he saw he was no longer alone. A crowd of people had formed a rough circle around him, appearing as if out of nowhere, though that could not possibly have been the case. He must have been so engrossed in studying the locket that he had neither seen nor heard them approach. They were dressed in little more than rags, feet bare, skin grimy and rank. The sour stench of them washed over him and almost made him choke. Their faces were expressionless, their eyes unreadable, and there was something about the way they stood, silent and motionless, that he found more threatening than if they had screamed at him and chased him from their camp. It was all Kelvin could do to stop himself from running, to plough straight into them and pray he could force his way through before they could react. Something, some survival instinct, told him that would not be a smart move. Better to explain why he was there, play up the emotion, the missing wife angle, and trust they would respond in a suitably sympathetic way.

He raised a hand in greeting and managed to force his dust-dry mouth into what he hoped was a friendly smile. Before he had chance to say a word, the crowd parted in front of him and a young boy stepped forward. He was, Kelvin realised, the first child he had seen in the camp. The others were adults, from older teenagers right through to very old, some so frail and decrepit they looked barely able to stand.

"Hello," he said.

The child, maybe six or seven, regarded him with an intense

solemnity that in other circumstances would have struck Kelvin as amusing on such a young face. "This is our home," he said, his voice as grave as his expression. "Why are you here?"

Kelvin hesitated momentarily, not quite sure how to respond. It was a simple enough question, but the way it had been phrased struck him as odd. Children did not use such clipped, stilted language. He wondered if the kid was a little bit backward. It would not have surprised him; everyone here looked a few cards short of a deck.

"I'm sorry," he said. "I didn't mean to invade your privacy. I'm looking for my wife. She's run away from home and I'm worried about her. She hasn't been well."

"I see," the child answered, nodding like an old sage. "And why did you believe you would find her here in this camp?"

There it was again. That oddly heightened way of speaking. Kelvin broke out in a sweat which had nothing to do with the heat. He pulled the locket from his jeans and held it out towards the boy. "I found this in the grass. It belongs to my wife."

The child stared at it. "Now I understand. You are talking about Mary."

"She's here?"

"Yes."

"Then take me to her, please. I need to know she's okay."

"You are certain that is what you want?"

"Of course I am! Now will you please let me see her?"

The child said nothing. Instead he glanced sideways towards the crowd, and two old woman suddenly reached out and grabbed Kelvin by the arms, forcing him to his knees before he had time to react. "Get your bloody hands off me," he shouted, momentarily taken

115

aback. The women looked feeble but they were incredibly strong, their fingers like steel bands digging into his flesh. "I'm warning you, get your —"

"Be quiet," the boy said, and Kelvin's voice was abruptly silenced. It wasn't that he had stopped talking. His mouth still moved but the words could not be heard, like someone on the television when the sound had been turned off. Now he was no longer nervous; he was scared in a way he had never thought possible. It was the first time in his life he had ever been completely incapacitated, powerless to break free of the hands which held him, unable even to call for help. Whatever fate the boy and his freakish companions had in mind for him, there was nothing Kelvin could do to resist.

The child leant forward until their faces almost touched. Their eyes met and Kelvin found he could not tear his gaze away. It was like falling into a deep, warm pool. His fear evaporated. He felt safe now, protected, with no reason to be afraid. The touch of the sun and breeze on his skin, the sounds of traffic in the distance, all faded away until his mind was empty of everything save the boy's words.

"Your voice drowns out what your heart is trying to tell you," the child said, his tone soft yet utterly compelling. "Consider this. If you could have anything in the world, anything at all, no matter how impossible, what would it be? Believe me when I tell you I have the power to grant you that which you most desire. But think long and hard first, Kelvin. Dreams can so easily turn into nightmares if one is not careful."

With that, he turned and walked away. Kelvin, head whirling, dimly felt himself being hauled to his feet and marched away from the camp. At first he thought he was being allowed to leave, but then he saw the two old women were leading him towards a derelict old building. He struggled and started to yell, barely registering that his voice had returned, but to no avail. It was as futile as trying to turn back the tide. One of the women pulled open a wooden door in the front of the building and Kelvin was hurled inside, struggling and failing to keep his balance and cracking his head as he fell. White light filled his mind and he must have lost consciousness, for the next thing he knew he was looking up at Tanya, her face a mask of concern.

"Where - where are we?" he gasped. "How did we get out?"

"Oh, Kelvin," she said, and started to cry. "I'm sorry. I should have listened to you and stayed in the car, but when you didn't come back I was so worried."

"Wait," he said, trying to sit up, alarmed at the way his head throbbed and spun when he moved it. His fingers touched his forehead and came away red. The ground beneath his back felt damp and hard. Kelvin looked around slowly. A wedge of light from where the door did not quite meet its frame was the only illumination, but it was enough for him to see they were in a small room with no windows. The air was dank and faintly earthy. Kelvin, remembering the old building he had been led towards, guessed it once must have been used as a horse shelter. He got up slowly, brushing off Tanya's attempts to help him, and pressed an eye against a crack in the door. Fuck. The two old crones were standing rigidly, as if to attention, right outside. Beyond them the camp looked deserted again. Something really fucking weird was going on here, he thought. Not so much that business with the kid. Okay, so Kelvin had felt like he was being hypnotised, but that was probably just the heat and the past few anxious, sleepless nights catching up with him. No, it was the way all those people had stood around in a zombified stupor like something out a George Romero film, and the way they appeared as if out of nowhere and vanished just as quickly.

"Kelvin, what's going on? I'm frightened."

He moved away from the door, knowing he should have been thinking about Tanya more than himself and feeling bad that he hadn't. After all it was his fault that she was caught up in this. He should never have asked her to come with him, and wouldn't have if he had not been so much of a coward. He put his hands on her shoulders and pulled her towards him, aching at the way her body trembled.

"I'm sorry," he said. "The people who live here didn't take kindly to me snooping about the place. But at least I've found Mary. They told me she was here."

"Oh, well, that's okay, then." Tanya's bitter tone softened. "Sorry."

"Don't be. I shouldn't have dragged you into this."

"I mean it, Kelvin. I'm just being selfish. I know you've been worried about Mary and I'm glad she's all right. I just wish we could get out of this place."

"You should have stayed in the car, like I told you."

She looked away. "I know, I know. But I only got out to have a look. Then I saw this man. He told me you had asked him to fetch me, so I went with him. Then he said I was to wait here. I can't believe I was so stupid. I knew something wasn't right. I should have run away right there and then."

"He wouldn't have let you," Kelvin said, realising from the way Tanya suddenly went rigid that he had said the wrong thing.

"What are they going to do to us?"

"Nothing, I shouldn't think." It was better to lie. "Probably keep us locked in here for a while just to scare us, then let us go. I told them the police knew we were coming here, so I doubt they would be stupid enough to do anything more than that."

Tanya buried her face in his shoulder. "God, I hope you're right."

The smell of her so close to him was intoxicating. How many times had they been like this, only for Kelvin to hold back out of misplaced loyalty to Mary? He cursed his own rotten luck. Now that he had finally come to terms with the fact that he no longer had a marriage, now that he no longer had to worry about fidelity, he was locked up in a camp full of fucking weirdos when he should be in bed making love to Tanya, a long-time dream come true. What was it that crazy boy had said? That he could give Kelvin anything he wanted. Well, he wanted Tanya more than anything else in the world. No point wishing for his daughter back or for his marriage to be saved. It would take more than a kid to pull that brace of miracles off.

It was as if Tanya sensed what was going on in his mind. Her arms encircled him, holding him tight, and she moaned beneath her breath as he grew stiff. Her face turned to his and after a fleeting hesitation, he kissed her. Her lips parted and her tongue slid into his mouth. His defences were breached by an onslaught of desire and his hands slid down to cup her breasts. The world around him ceased to exist. He was aware only of the soft feel of her, the warm moistness of her mouth, the electrifying touch of her hands as she undid his zip and slid them inside. The door could open at any time, but he was beyond caring. They slid to the ground, Kelvin groaning deeply as Tanya twisted and turned, kissing his erect penis before sliding her lips over it. He closed his eyes and shuddered as wave after wave of

119

pure pleasure coursed through him. This is it, he thought deliriously, this is what I want.

Which is when his world went insane.

SIXTEEN

Captain stood behind the crowd, out of sight, and watched with a smirk on his face as the woman pleaded for her life. Oh, she'd been full of herself when he had opened the car door and told her he was taking her to her boyfriend, or whoever the fuck he was. All airs and graces, she was, demanding to know what Captain thought he was doing and what the hell was going on. Asking for a good slap, she'd been, a good solid backhand to shut her up good and proper, but he'd held his temper in check. The boy in his head made it clear he would not be happy if Captain harmed the girl. Even so, the little tramp had started snivelling when they reached the camp and the kid appeared to her. He could see glistening tracks of the tears on her cheeks as the child asked her about her dreams. If it had been up to Captain, he would have just given her a bloody good seeing to and sent her on her way. What in Christ's name did empty-headed kids like her know about dreams, anyway?

But of course it wasn't up to him. The kid was planning something, some trick or other, and Captain knew he would find out what it was if he waited long enough. And so he stood there, his mind a long way away, only vaguely aware of the conversation between the boy and the snotty-nosed bitch, and thinking, not for the first time, that he could murder a flagon of Strongbow and a couple of straight whiskys right then.

I have no further use for this one. Deal with her.

Fuck, he wished the kid wouldn't do that, speak right into his head. He didn't do it very often, but when he did it never failed to make Captain jump. He elbowed his way through the crowd, pushing

121

the dull-eyed morons out of his way. As the girl saw him her face lit up and she stumbled to her feet, ran to him and threw her arms around him with manic force. Captain, who wondered what in Christ's name was going on, almost pushed her away. Then a whisper in his mind let him in on the secret.

"Oh, Kelvin" she cried. "Christ, I was so scared. Who are these people?"

"Don't worry," he said. "You're safe now. No one's going to hurt you."

His voice belonged to that Kelvin. The words came from the child. Captain realised he was no longer in control of his actions. He was the kid's puppet again. Not that he was bothered. This time was special, oh yes. He was going to have some fun.

"Please, can we get out of here?"

"Sure we can." He took her hand and led her away, sensing her reluctance as he took her deeper into the camp but squeezing her hand reassuringly. When they arrived at one of the larger tents he pushed the flap open and led her inside.

"Kelvin, wait. What are you doing? I thought we were getting out of here."

"Shut your fucking mouth," Captain said, feeling the child release his control over him, and simultaneously understanding what he had to do. How he achieved it was up to him and he was determined to make sure the opportunity did not go to waste. A thrill of anticipation ran through him when he saw the look on the girl's face change from concern to pure undisguised fear. He put both hands on her shoulders and pushed her to the ground. A scream died on her lips as he forced himself on top of her, one hand clamping itself around her mouth, the other fumbling at her skirt. The little bitch bucked and rolled furiously, trying to throw him off. When that didn't work she bit his hand, but the pain barely registered. The girl began to moan, then to whimper. Her terror only served to stoke his fire, and he entered her with a force that made him gasp. Before long Captain was where he wanted to be, lost in oblivion, albeit an oblivion of a different kind. He was so carried away that, later, he would not remember the moment when his hands tightened around her throat and squeezed the life out of her.

When it was over, Captain rolled off and staggered to his feet, breathless and shaking. He looked down at the body and tried to figure out how long it had been since he'd experienced this kind of release without the use of his palm. Too long, he concluded. Maybe he should have made this one last a little bit longer, hitched a few more rides while he had the chance. But this was no time for regrets, he thought, hearing the soft scrunch of footsteps on the grass outside the tent. He had work to do.

-SEVENTEEN-

Martyn collapsed against the rock, the trembling worse now than it had been after he saw the girl's body dumped the in river. For one awful moment, when he'd felt the hand on his shoulder, heard the gruff voice telling him not to move, he had known beyond doubt that it was over for him, that his corpse was destined to hit the water next.

"Sorry lad," Tom said, a touch sheepishly.

"Jeez," Martyn gasped. "Don't ever do that to me again."

"I said I was sorry. It was only meant to be a bit of fun."

"Fun? *Fun*?" Martyn shook his head angrily, then reined in his temper. At another time it might well have been a bit of fun. But of course Tom did not know what was going on here, had no idea what Martyn had seen. And so Martyn told him, watching the other's expression change from mock-contrite to serious. By the time he had finished with the telling, Tom's face had grown extremely grim indeed.

Tom lit one of his cigarettes and lowered himself to the ground, where he sat opposite Martyn so that the boulder shielded them both from the view of anyone in the camp who happened to glance their way.

"Anyway, how did you manage to find me?" Martyn asked.

"Rhiannon told me. She ... she sees things. I've learned over the years never to doubt her ." Tom sighed. "Just as well I *did* find you. This is a bad business. You did the right thing by keeping yourself hidden. These sound like extremely unpleasant people."

"Who do you think they are?"

"No way of knowing," Tom said. "Could be just an ordinary

bunch of folks too high on drink or drugs. Maybe they got carried away with something, some game that went wrong, and that poor girl paid for it.

"You hear so many strange stories these days," Tom continued. "Anything is possible." He stubbed his cigarette out in the grass and immediately lit another. "What were you planning to do next?"

"Wait until I could leave without being seen, then call the police."

Tom pulled a face. "Can't argue with the first part. Forget the second, though."

"They just killed a woman! We have to report it."

"We don't *have* to do any such thing, lad. If you want to survive on the streets the one lesson you need to learn is, never get involved. You can't afford to."

"You got involved with me, didn't you? You saved my life."

"True," Tom said, looking uncomfortable. "The difference there was, you still had a life to save. That poor lass is gone whether we call the police or not."

"I don't care. What if we didn't report it and they killed someone else? It would be our fault. And there's something else, something I just remembered. There was a man here. I saw him just before they threw the body into the river. I don't know what was going on, but it looked like he was being held prisoner."

"And what makes you think that?"

Martyn described the way the man had been frogmarched into the shelter, recalled with a shudder how the two old women had guarded the door like two standing stones. "That's why I couldn't move. In case they saw me."

125

"Well, there was nobody around when I got here," Tom said. "To be honest, there was no sign of life in the camp at all. Looked like the place had been deserted."

"There's people in there, all right. Take my word for it."

"I don't doubt you," Tom said, peering carefully around the boulder. "We'd best get out of here before there's any more trouble."

"Wait a minute —"

"We can argue about calling the police later. Personally, I'd rather be as far away from this place as possible before I start worrying about anything else."

"But what about the man I told you about? The prisoner."

"We don't know that for sure."

"Oh, come off it." While he knew that Tom was right, that hanging around even a second longer than necessary would be foolish, not to mention downright risky, neither did Martyn feel he could simply abandon the man. After all, he owed his own life to a stranger. If Tom had not intervened Martyn would have been seriously hurt or possibly killed. There had been nobody else around to help him. Of course what Martyn had seen here may well have been a sick game of some kind. He could not begin to imagine what might be going on in the heads of people who could kill a girl, accidentally or otherwise, then dispose of the evidence so callously. But to his mind it had all been played too straight to be anything other than deadly serious. "We can't just leave him there."

"Whoever he is, he's no concern of ours. If you're that worried, we'll do what you suggested and call the police. Anonymously. Let them sort it out."

"What if they don't believe us and something happens to him?"

"You're not going to let go of this, are you?"

"I can't. Anyway, you know I'm right."

"I still think it's a bloody stupid thing to do." Tom sighed heavily. "But okay."

"Thanks, Tom."

Trouble was, having gotten his own way, Martyn suddenly felt nervous. His stomach fluttered and his breath turned short and shallow. It was easy to talk about helping, but as the reality started to hit home he wondered whether they were doing the right thing after all. All it would take was for someone in the camp to look their way, or return to check on the prisoner, and they would really be in the shit. "Let's get it over with," he said, hating the tremble in his voice and hoping Tom hadn't noticed.

"You stay here," Tom told him. "Less chance of one of us being seen."

"No way. This was my idea. I'm coming with you."

"Goddammit. For someone so young you can be a stubborn little sod."

"Maybe I've had to grow up fast," Martyn said, struck for the first time by how true that was. He did not feel like a kid any longer. He felt in control, and he liked it.

"Suit yourself. Just be quiet and if I tell you to run, you run like hell, okay?"

Martyn nodded, waited for Tom as he peered towards the camp one final time, then followed him out from behind the boulder and on to the gravel path. Every step they took was a deafening crunch. He let Tom lead the way towards the shelter, his own eyes nailed to the camp, so jittery that even the slightest shift of shadow, the merest ruffle of canvas, translated into an imminent threat of detection. They left the path and walked across the field, feet now cushioned by the grass, but it made no difference. Martyn knew, simply knew, they were not going to make it, was so convinced of the fact that it came as a shock when he realised the shelter was only a few yards ahead of them. Tom reached out to take his elbow and steered him to the side of the ramshackle building so that it shielded them from the camp. Martyn, legs threatening to give way beneath him, leant back against the breezeblocks. The rough texture of the concrete against his spine reminded him that he had left his rucksack at the boulder. That was the least of his worries. He'd pick it up on the way back. Assuming he got the chance.

Tom raised a finger to his lips, then pointed it at Martyn, indicating he wanted the boy to stay put, rolling his eyes theatrically when Martyn shook his head. Then the older man crept to the edge of the wall and looked around it. He gave the thumbs-up and stepped out, with Martyn close enough behind to almost touch him. They studied the door. It was old and battered and painted black, held shut by a single bolt midway up. From inside they could hear a low moaning, that and another sound, something wet and breathy that Martyn could not identify. He watched intently as Tom worked the bolt free with heart-stopping care, pausing whenever the rusting metal gave the tiniest squeal of protest. Finally the last inch of the bar slid from its socket, and Tom used the flat of his hand to prevent the door from moving. He looked at Martyn, nodded, then eased the door open, cringing as the hinges groaned their disapproval. A ripe earthy smell assaulted them when they stepped inside, blinking as their vision adjusted to the darkness. The strange sounds they had heard from outside were louder, more hurried, emanating from ground level. Martyn gazed down. For a few confused seconds he was not sure what he was looking at but, just as one of those Magic Eye pictures made sense if you stared at it for long enough, so too an image finally emerged in the dark room.

It was almost enough to make him gag.

The man he had seen being led here lay on the packed dirt floor, mouth open, eyes clamped shut. His jeans had been pulled down to his ankles and a grey-haired woman knelt over him, face buried in his groin. He moaned deeply, writhing in time with the frantic bobbing motions of the woman's head, hands at his side clenching and unclenching like he was trying to dig into the ground. Martyn gawped. He hardly felt it when Tom put a hand on his chest and tried to push him out the door, but the shove made him stagger backwards a couple of steps, whereupon he regained his balance and looked on as if in a trance as Tom set about breaking up the man and woman. It was like watching the blackest of comedies, the kind that made you laugh even while it sickened you. First Tom grabbed the woman's shoulder and shook it roughly, but to no avail. Then he caught hold of her hair and tugged at it. Again it made no difference at all. Thinking that maybe he should try to help, Martyn stepped forward and, ignoring Tom's helpless glare, knelt on the ground and used both hands in an attempt to push the woman away.

Her head swivelled and fixed him with one baleful eye. For a split-second he saw her grin around the man's saliva-oiled penis, then her hand, which was resting on the floor beside him, curled into a fist that planted itself deep in Martyn's stomach. It happened so quickly he did not even see the punch coming. The next thing he knew he was

129

in a crumpled heap by the wall, unable to move, his belly a mass of fire, his lungs a vacuum. He tried desperately to suck down air, but there was some kind of obstruction in his throat. A veil of tears blurred his vision, so he barely saw Tom take a step back before lashing out with his foot, catching the woman square in the head. She began to shriek, the noise bouncing off the walls, undulating like a siren and just as ear-piercing. Tom kicked at her again and Martyn, wiping his eyes with the back of his hand, winced as her nose burst and a torrent of blood cascaded down her face. It was enough to silence the scream, but not to stop her. The man forgotten, she snarled at Tom, twisting her head so that his next kick missed her. She leapt to her feet with an agility that belied her age and advanced on Tom, hissing like a cat and lashing out wildly with both fists. It was the first time Martyn had seen his friend fight. He was impressed. Tom blocked the punches with ease and delivered a few of his own. Each was aimed at the woman's face and was smack on target. Her head snapped from side to side as blow after blow landed. The woman was in her fifties or sixties at least, yet she was withstanding the kind of punishment that would have brought a champion boxer to his knees.

Tom grew visibly tired: his punches carried less force and he staggered whenever he blocked one of hers. Just as it seemed he was about to go down, an opening appeared and he seized on it, swinging his fist in a wide sweeping arc which connected with the point of her chin. Her head snapped back, her knees buckled and she toppled forward, her forehead slamming into the wall close to Martyn with a noise like an eggshell cracking. She slid the rest of the way to the floor, a smear of blood on the concrete marking her progress, and then she no longer moved.

Tom, chest heaving, weaving unsteadily, looked at her and then at Martyn. "You all right?" he asked in a voice that did not sound like his own.

Martyn nodded.

"Good," Tom said, then rubbed a hand across his face. "What the hell was that all about? Must have been sixty if she was a day, but she fought like a thing possessed. And that ... other business. Jesus Christ almighty."

Which reminded Martyn that maybe they should check on the man, who had neither moved nor made a sound. Stomach muscles spasming alarmingly, he crawled across the floor until he reached the supine form. The stranger's eyes were wide open and unblinking. Martyn thought he was dead until he noticed the rise and fall of his chest, shallow but visible nonetheless. He could only imagine that the man, who was younger than Martyn's father, had been drugged. Otherwise why else would he have allowed that ancient old bag to ... to do what she'd been doing to him?

"Can you hear me?" Martyn asked.

The man's eyes closed, then opened, very slowly, and his tongue ran around his lips. He squinted up at Martyn and shook his head a few times like he was trying to clear it, then began to sit up. The effort proved too much for him and he flopped back to the ground. "Where's Tanya?" he croaked. "What have you bastards done with her?"

"Hey now," said Tom, standing behind Martyn and helping the boy to his feet. "Mind your language in front of the lad. He's seen enough as it is. We don't know anything about Tanya. We've nothing to do with the people who brought you here."

"Then who are you?"

"Friends," Tom said. "You look as if you could do with some right now."

"Huh?" The man must have become aware of his dishevelled state for he reddened and reached down, awkwardly tugging his underwear and jeans up his legs. "Just what the fuck has been going on?"

"That can wait," Tom answered. "Thing is, there's a bunch of very unpleasant people just a few yards away and I'd rather get out of here before they find us."

"But who are —"

"Later," Tom snapped. "We have to get out of here. Now. Can you stand?"

"Don't know." The man rolled on to his side and pushed himself up to his knees, weaving slightly. Tom grabbed him by one arm and nodded at Martyn to take the other. Between them they managed to hoist him to his feet. "Thanks," he said, frowning when he saw the unconscious woman by the wall. "Who the hell's she?"

"If that's not Tanya," Tom said slowly, "I don't think you want to know."

"Of course it's not Tanya! She's ... oh, forget it. Tell me later. My head's hurting so badly I can't think straight. Feels like I've spent the last couple of days drinking."

"If you have, it would explain a lot," said Tom. "You got a name, by the way?"

"Sorry. It's Kelvin. Kelvin Denny."

"Right. I'm Tom. The upshot is, both of us have put our heads in the noose good and proper for you. I guess you can thank Martyn for that. He's got more of a conscience than me, talked me out of leaving you here."

Martyn looked away, embarrassed.

"So you owe us both," Tom continued. "There's a gate maybe fifty yards from here. If we can get through that without anyone seeing us, then we should be okay. Straight up the path to the main road. There'll be cars about, and I doubt anyone would risk coming after us in front of potential witnesses. Now listen carefully because this is important. Once we walk out of this door we don't stop until I say so, understand?"

Martyn nodded, saw Kelvin do the same.

"Good," said Tom. He let go of Kelvin's arm and crossed to the door, looking out quickly in the direction of the camp. "Coast's clear. Follow me and stay close. You see me start to run, you do the same, and for God's sake try to keep up."

Crossing the field a second time was every inch as nerve-wracking as the first. The camp still looked deserted, but then again it had done just before he saw the two old women frog marching Kelvin to the shelter, followed swiftly by the bearded man and he remembered with terrifying clarity what had happened after that. At least by now the sun had dipped behind the hills surrounding Morfa, diffusing the light and deepening the shadows, which would undoubtedly work in their favour. The air had grown cooler but Martyn was sweating. When they passed through the field gate it felt like a monumental victory to him. True, they were not quite home and dry yet, but they had surely put the most dangerous part behind them. Martyn paused at the boulder only long enough to reach down and grab his rucksack. When he straightened he almost walked into Kelvin, who had stopped and was looking back towards the camp.

133

"Keep going," Martyn hissed. "We're still not safe."

"Wait," Kelvin said. "It's her!"

Martyn followed his gaze but could see nothing. Before he had a chance to say a word, Kelvin was off, marching back through the gate and heading straight for the first row of tents. Martyn looked around desperately. Tom had his back to them and was a few yards ahead, making his way to the tyre depot. Not daring to make a sound and with no other way of attracting Tom's attention, Martyn trotted after him. Tom disappeared around the side of the depot and was busying himself with lighting a cigarette by the time Martyn caught up. "Better wait for our friend Kelvin," Tom said, blowing smoke.

"He's gone back to the camp."

"What?"

"I couldn't stop him. He said he'd seen someone. Somebody he knew."

Tom's face darkened. "The bloody idiot. What the hell's wrong with him?"

"It must have been that Tanya he was talking about," Martyn said.

"I don't care who it was," Tom snapped back. He jerked back his coat sleeve and glared at his watch. "If he wants to get himself into trouble straight after we've gotten him out of it, that's his problem. He's got two minutes, then we're out of here."

In less than half that time they heard scuffling footsteps and a low murmuring voice from around the corner. Tom gently pushed Martyn against the depot wall, then stood with his fist clenched and raised. He lowered it with a snort which could have signified relief or exasperation when Kelvin staggered into view, his arm around a blonde woman whose head was slumped forward. Her hands were clasped at her chest, holding something small and pale. A doll, Martyn realised with mild disbelief.

"Sorry," Kelvin gasped. "But I had to go back. I couldn't leave her."

"Well, at least you're back in one piece," said Tom. "This must be Tanya."

"No, this is Mary. My wife. Tanya's a ... a friend of ours. She's still in there but I couldn't find her. If Mary hadn't been wandering about I wouldn't have found her, either." He shuddered. "To tell you the truth, I was going to leave Mary with you and go back to look for Tanya, but there's something really fucking strange about that place. One minute it looks deserted, the next it's full of people. Weird people."

"Tell us about it," Martyn said. "What's wrong with your wife? Is she ill?"

"She's been through a lot. I'll explain later."

"Good idea," Tom said, dropping what remained of his cigarette and crushing it with his boot. "I know you're worried about your friend, but going back for her isn't the best of ideas. We were going to call the police in any event. Let them deal with it. For now I just want to put this damned place well behind us as quickly as possible."

Kelvin patted his jeans pocket. "No problem there. My car's parked just a little way up the main road. I can have us back in Swansea in next to no time."

"Thank God for a little good luck for once," Tom said. He looked as though he was going to add something, but instead he frowned and shook his head.

"What is it?" Martyn asked.

"Nothing. Come on - let's get a move on."

Tom led the way up the path while Martyn helped Kelvin with his wife, who was so unresponsive she could easily have been asleep on her feet. She did not speak, nor did she seem aware of her surroundings, and if the two of them had not been holding her up, Martyn thought, she would simply have collapsed to the ground. Whatever had happened to her, it must have been pretty bad. There were a million questions he wanted to ask but he kept quiet, aware that this was neither the place nor the time.

When they reached the car, a late model Ford Escort, they placed Mary in the back seat where she sat dead to the world, the doll still clasped to her chest. As they did, Martyn was chilled by the look in Kelvin's eyes, a look that went beyond mere sadness into a realm of despair that he could not even begin to imagine. He went around to the other side of the car and sat in the back, as far away from Mary as he could get, ashamed of himself for not wanting to be close to her but equally unable to do anything about it.

Kelvin drove steadily enough, considering what he had been through, but Martyn could see his eyes in the rearview mirror, flicking nervously between the road and Mary. He took a different route back to Swansea from the route Martyn's bus had followed, rolling to a halt alongside the first telephone box they passed. Kelvin switched off the engine, pulled the keys from the ignition and opened his door. Then he seemed to have second thoughts, and turned to face Tom. "Look, I'd rather not have to talk to the police if I don't have to. Long story. Do you think you could call for me?"

"In for a penny," Tom said. "Tell me what she looks like, what she's wearing."

Kelvin did, and Martyn went icy cold.

Tom turned round in his seat, a questioning look on his face. Martyn nodded and Tom's eyes closed briefly. "Right," he said airily. "This won't take a minute."

"Then what?" Kelvin asked. "I can't go home. Those people who had Mary, they may have found out from her where we live. I don't want them coming after us."

"Don't worry," Tom said. "I know a safe place. They'll never find us there."

And then he was gone from the car, leaving Martyn dreading the moment when they finally reached safety and the explanations started, when they would have to tell Kelvin that calling the police was a waste of time. Because his description of Tanya matched that of the girl whose body had been dumped in the river.

-EIGHTEEN-

Captain seethed. His fists curled and uncurled with frustration as he watched the car pull away. They were letting the bastards go! He could not believe it, simply could not fucking believe it. He'd been convinced the kid had been up to something, first of all by tricking Mary into coming with them, then by playing games with her husband and his bit on the side. Okay, so the bimbo was dead and that was fine by him. Crazy old Alice was lifeless too, lying in a crumpled heap in the shelter, forehead smashed. Still, she'd gone out with a smile on her face, judging by what Captain had seen.

And he'd seen it all. Every last bit of it. Watched as the boy hid behind the boulder like nobody could see him. Watched as that tall fucker in the trench coat joined him. Oh yes, he remembered that one all right, had been tempted to deal with him right there and then, except the child had made it clear with a single vivid image what he would do to Captain if he so much as moved. So instead he'd been forced to stand there, watching the whole fucking story unfold before him, seeing what by rights he should never have seen, a film brought to him courtesy of the child's magic.

He'd been pissed off, sure he had, but he'd sort of assumed they were just waiting for the right moment. So not daring to do otherwise, he'd waited as patiently as he could as events played themselves out in his mind. Captain had even managed a laugh when Crazy Alice started blowing Kelvin, who had absolutely no idea that the mouth wrapped around his dick was toothless and three times as old as he thought.

And then it was over and all three of them were getting away.

Worse, Kelvin had been allowed to come back for his wife, having seen her even though everyone else in the camp was invisible to him. The car had driven off and that had been that, leaving Captain furious and starting to wonder if the child was just a fucking nutcase after all.

As soon as he thought that, he wished he hadn't. He was in no doubt the kid had power. Serious power. The kind that could make people see what wasn't there, and see right past what was. The power to make you spill your guts about your dreams and then to give them to you, admittedly for a heavy price. Judging by the others, who were little more than slack-jawed fuckwits trudging about the camp, carrying out the child's silent and unfathomable instructions, Captain was lucky. He still had a mind of his own and he was still allowed those wondrous glimpses of oblivion. So it was pretty fucking stupid of him to risk all that by even thinking the child had a few screws loose in his head. He just hoped the kid hadn't picked up the thought.

Which he had. Of course he had. But, to Captain's immense relief, he did not seem too bothered. If anything, the kid found it amusing. He certainly seemed pleased with himself. Everything, he told Captain, was going to plan. Then, without saying a word, he revealed exactly what that plan was. One minute it was a mystery; then, in the blink of an eye, Captain knew everything. How the kid had manipulated events in order to bring those four bastards together, and why they'd been allowed to leave. Where the child's army were going and what they were seeking, the ultimate prize at the end of it. And it was one hell of a prize, he thought, marvelling at the sheer unbelievable scale of what they were about to embark on. For a second his confidence wavered, but then he remembered the rat and the girl in the tent and he was satisfied again that he could do anything. He only had to

139

remain loyal to the child.

And there was absolutely no fucking doubt about that.

Captain grinned as he surveyed the cars and vans dotted around the camp. He had wondered why the kid had brought so many of them, considering he only ever got around on foot, that and some other means of travel which Captain could not even begin to figure out. Now he knew. It wasn't so much the vehicles they needed as what was inside them. Captain could almost feel the heat on his skin, taste the acrid smoke.

Not long now, he thought, before the heat and the smoke are for real.

-NINETEEN-

They had left Kelvin alone, which was fine by him. Company was the last thing he wanted right then. He stared at his face in the window, the soft glow of the candles which lit the room reshaping and shadowing his features so that he barely recognised himself. Beyond the mirrored image there was nothing but black. Old Town, or at least what he could see of it, was a huddle of dark shapes only barely defined by the deeper darkness which surrounded them. There were no lights, save that of the moon and the flickering stars which appeared unusually vivid.

Old Town. A place which did not exist. Yet it did. He could see it, was a part of it. Kelvin tried to figure out how that could be, but gave up when he realised he would never really understand. Tom had tried to explain when they had first arrived, Kelvin nodding in the right places as if taking it all in his stride. Truth was, he didn't understand a word of it. Didn't really care, either. He had lost too much.

They had told Kelvin everything. About the body being dumped in the river. About the old woman in the shelter and what she had been doing to him. He had been confused by that, and disgusted, but it had not really registered. All he could think about was Tanya. Feisty, selfish Tanya. Demanding Tanya. Beautiful, tender, loving Tanya. Dead now, and it was his fault. No question of that. He should never have got her involved in the first place. He sighed deeply and rubbed his eyes.

First Jessica. Now Tanya. The fact that he had succeeded in finding Mary, which was what it had all been about in the first place, was no consolation. She might just as well be lost to him, too. Hadn't made a sound since he'd found her in the camp. In the car she had closed her eyes and rocked her head slowly back and forth as if listening to a lullaby that no one else could hear, that pathetic plastic doll clasped to her chest all the while.

And of course he could not forget what he had done. The weird kid had told him he could have anything he wanted, and what he had wanted was Tanya. He had put her ahead of his wife and his daughter and he could never forgive himself for that. And to top it off, he thought grimly, the Tanya the child had given him had not been real. It had all been a sick joke, that was all. Kelvin shuddered when he tried to imagine what might have happened had he asked to have his daughter returned to him instead.

It was like a nightmare. Except he knew it was real. As crazy as the world had suddenly become, it was the waking world nonetheless. He only vaguely remembered driving into Swansea, following Tom's directions until they'd arrived at a rundown part of the city Kelvin had never seen before. They had dumped the Escort in a side street and, more or less carrying Mary between them, had staggered down a lane until Tom was satisfied there was nobody else about. Then he had simply stepped through a wall.

Not a gap in the wall but the wall itself. It was that sight, more than anything else which had happened to him, that had almost flipped Kelvin over the brink. He had felt his mind come alarmingly close to snapping. A man walking through a wall! It was not only impossible, but hilarious. He had wanted to laugh, and to keep laughing until the sound of it drowned out everything else in his head. And he may very well have done so had Martyn not tugged at his arm and told him to get a move on.

142

The rest of their journey had been normal in comparison, save for the fact that the streets had been deserted and the houses had looked all wrong, as if they were somehow too new to be as old as their architecture implied. Kelvin had found himself disturbed more by the absence of the ordinary than by any suggestion of the extraordinary. Where were the cars, the people, for Christ's sake? What about all the litter and dogshit and graffiti? And why was the place so quiet? It was like a morgue. He had said nothing, suspecting sensory overload. Too much information too quickly for his still-hazy brain to absorb. It had taken all his concentration simply to walk in a straight line after Tom and not to allow his grip on Mary to slacken. By the time they'd reached wherever it was they were going, he'd felt physically and mentally drained.

Not that he felt much better now. If anything, he felt worse. He had a death on his conscience, and not the faintest idea of what he was going to do about his wife. The girl Rhiannon had taken a look at her, only to say that Mary was beyond her help. Whatever had happened had scarred her so deeply that she had retreated into some inner sanctuary where nothing else could harm her. Kelvin had told them about the baby and they'd been sympathetic, but it made no difference. What Rhiannon had been telling him, albeit as tactfully as possible, Kelvin thought sourly, was that his wife had gone crazy. It had only been a matter of time, but even so he felt truly sad now that the moment had come. He had loved her once. Still did, only not in the same way.

She was sleeping in the next room, curled up like a child the last time Kelvin had checked, refusing to relinquish her hold on the doll. The other three were in a room across the hallway, talking quietly. Maybe he would join them. Not yet, though. He still did not feel

143

much like company. There was too much left to think about. Like how to explain all this to the police. He hadn't wanted to talk to Miles after they'd fled the camp, not until he could think straight, in case he gave the detective the wrong idea about Tanya. Or the right idea, more like. Some grieving father he would have seemed had he let slip his fantasy of screwing the babysitter.

It would be easy to call Miles, to tell him everything that had happened and let the police go to the camp and make whatever enquiries they had to make. Problem was, they might not believe Kelvin's story. For all he knew the camp was gone, with nothing left behind to show it had ever been there. And should word of his alleged affair have got all around the office, as he feared, who was to say the finger of suspicion would not be pointed at him? He could not handle that. Quite apart from the fact that he was innocent - no, Christ, he was one of the victims - he still had Mary to think about. He could hardly leave her. Not because Tanya was dead, but because Mary so desperately needed his help.

Shit, he thought. *What a mess.*

The prospect of companionship was suddenly a welcome one. Kelvin turned away from the window and walked out of the room, crossing the corridor quietly so as not to disturb Mary. The three of them looked up as he entered, their conversation ending abruptly. He had the uncomfortable feeling they had been talking about him.

"How is she?" Rhiannon asked.

"Don't know. Haven't checked for a while."

"Good idea," Tom said. "Best to let her sleep."

They sounded genuine, but Kelvin wondered if they were merely humouring him. He had been found, after all, with his pants around his ankles and his dick inside an old woman's mouth. Maybe they thought Mary was not the only one who was crazy. Not that he could do anything about it except sit around until daylight and try to work out in his mind how the hell he was going to sort this whole mess out.

Old Town, he had been told, provided its residents with all their needs. If that was true then Rhiannon's needs were basic, to say the least. There was no carpet on the floor and no furniture other than a table, two spoon-backed wooden chairs and a small sofa on which Martyn and Tom sat. Kelvin wondered what the people of Old Town did to pass the time if they all lived in conditions as spartan as this. They didn't go out much, that was for certain. He had seen not a soul on the street on his way here. Tom had said there were plenty of others around, but they tended to keep themselves to themselves. Most had spent a great part of their lives on the street and welcomed a roof over their heads. Kelvin could not imagine spending every day moping about in a place which should not even be here. Then again, neither could he have imagined a city that lived off people and offered them eternal life in return. He had accepted the idea with an ease that surprised him, and which he suspected was down to shock, but could not even begin to contemplate the enormity of the forces behind it.

Rhiannon had taken one of the chairs, and Kelvin lowered himself into the other with a small sigh of relief. It had been a long and tiring day. His muscles were feeling the strain. The dancing candlelight was hypnotic. He closed his eyes and rubbed them. When he opened them again he could see the others looking at him curiously. "What?" he demanded, feeling his frayed temper come close to snapping.

"Nothing," Tom said. "We're just trying to work something

out."

"Such as what?"

The three exchanged glances and then Tom spoke up again. "Such as whether there's more going on here than meets the eye. See, there have been a few coincidences around here of late and, to tell you the truth, I don't like it. One or two coincidences I can accept. It's part of life. But I'm not talking one or two."

"Sorry, you've lost me," Kelvin said.

"I've seen you before, for a start," said Tom. "In the subway by The Kingsway a few days ago. You were being accosted by a drunk. Scruffy fellow. Big beard."

Kelvin remembered. It had not really registered at the time. Just one of those things. But, yes, he remembered the drunk. And he remembered the tall figure who, for some reason, had frightened the bearded man away. "Yeah, okay, so I saw him," he said. "And now you mention it, I think I saw you, too. What's the big deal about that?"

"You don't understand," Martyn said "That drunk, he was the same one who beat me up. And he was at the camp. He was with them when they dumped the body in the river." The boy's face reddened and he looked down. "Sorry. I know Tanya was your friend. But he was there. I saw him. We both saw him, didn't we, Tom?"

"That we did. Something else you should know, Kelvin. What you told us earlier, about your wife trying to steal that baby. I saw that as well."

"Oh, for Christ's sake," Kelvin said angrily, rising to his feet. "I don't know what you're think you're playing at but, whatever it is, cut it out. It isn't funny."

"It's not meant to be funny," Tom said. "Now sit down. We've all had a rough day today. No point snapping at each other. We need to figure out what's going on."

Kelvin hesitated a moment, then sat back down. "Chances are, there's nothing going on. I think you're seeing something that isn't there. Okay, so there have been a couple of coincidences, but what are you suggesting? Some kind of conspiracy?"

"I'm not suggesting anything," Tom answered. "The point is, my life hasn't changed much in fifty years. Then it's turned upside-down, and I want to know why."

"Because life's like that. Even in a weird place like this."

"No," Tom said softly. He got up and stood at the window, looking out into the night. "Life isn't like that. My life, anyway. I can't help feeling there's something going on, something we don't know about but we're caught up in it all the same."

"Tom's right," said Rhiannon, her first words since Kelvin had entered the room. "You have to live in Old Town for quite some time to realise that nothing changes. One day is just like the next. Only people like Tom who go out into the world ever see anything different, and then only because they choose to."

A retort came to mind but Kelvin bit it back, not wanting to hurt Rhiannon's feelings. She had been kind to Mary, after all, even if there had been nothing she could do to help. In the short time he had known her she had struck him as a level-headed girl. What on earth she had gone through to end up in this living dead town was anyone's guess. Kelvin supposed the scars on her face had something to do with it, but he was not about to ask, sensing that the question would hardly be welcome.

"I know it's not easy for you to understand," Tom said. "Old

147

The Ragchild

Town takes quite a lot of getting used to, as I told young Martyn here only a short while ago. The longer you stay, the more familiar your way of life becomes until you reach the point - " He broke off and leaned towards the window. "Oh sweet Jesus," he whispered.

"What?" Rhiannon said. "What is it?"

Tom turned to face her. "Come and look for yourself."

They all did, standing beside Tom at the window, peering into the darkness to try to find out what had bothered him. At first Kelvin thought he was merely seeing a reflection of the candles, but then he realised the flickering flames he could see were too big for that.

In the distance, Old Town was burning. There was not only one fire but a whole host of them. Kelvin watched as flames erupted through the roof of a terraced house a few streets over and then rapidly spread to its neighbours. Smoke billowed. The sky began to glow orange. "What's going on?" he demanded. "I thought you said we'd be safe here."

Tom looked at him. "Nothing like this has happened before."

"Maybe it's not what we think," Rhiannon said, but she was clearly as worried as Tom. "Maybe someone started a fire and it got out of hand. Accidents happen."

"Not here they don't," Tom said gravely. "You start a fire and Old Town puts it out before it does any damage." He rubbed a hand across his face. "I don't understand it. Nobody here would want to cause any trouble. We all have too much to lose."

"What are we going to do?" said Martyn.

"I'll go outside and have a look, try to find out what's happening. You three stay here. It's safer. If the fire looks like heading this way, I'll come back and tell you."

148

"But you can't go on your own," Martyn insisted. "You could get hurt."

"Don't worry about me, lad. I can look after myself. Kelvin, it might be an idea if you tried to rouse Mary. We may have to move quickly."

Rhiannon stepped away from the window. "I'll see to her," she said, smiling apologetically at Kelvin. "I'd rather you went with Tom. Keep him out of trouble."

"Dammit, girl, I don't need anyone to hold my hand."

"It's all right," Kelvin said, aware of the debt he owed Tom. "I don't mind."

"Looks like I'm outvoted." Tom paused until Rhiannon had left then put a hand on Martyn's shoulder. "I'm counting on you to look after her. And Mary. The first sign of trouble, you make sure you get them out sharpish. Understand?"

Martyn nodded.

"Good lad. Right then, Kelvin. Let's go for a little stroll, shall we?"

But before they could move, Rhiannon ran into the room, looking distraught.

"Mary's gone

- TWENTY -

Mary ran through the pitch-dark streets as fast as she dared, not knowing where she was going but absolutely certain it would be unsafe to stop. Her chest was on fire and her arms ached from carrying Jessica, but that was a pain she could happily bear.

Finding herself here, without warning, had come as a shock. The last thing she remembered was being in the camp, where the strange little boy dressed in raggedy clothes had asked her what she wanted more than anything else in the world.

Mary had not hesitated in telling him she wanted her little girl back.

And the child, God bless him, had made it happen.

Even now, with panic nipping at her heels like a dog, she remembered clearly how she had felt when Jessica was returned to her. When that old woman stepped from the crowd and handed the baby to Mary, it was as if every happy moment she had missed out on in her life suddenly came to her at once, a tidal wave of emotion so immense she could not react. No tears of happiness, no burst of laughter. Just a shocked bewilderment which rapidly gave way to the most wonderfully intense joy.

She barely recalled the boy saying something about her soul. It was the last thing she knew until a few minutes ago, when she had suddenly found herself in a place she did not recognise, convinced that something dreadful was about to happen. Instinct had taken hold, spurring her into flight. Mary dashed along one road, then another, taking turnings at random, with only the moon to light the way. Apart from the sound of her footsteps, which seemed shockingly loud, it was so quiet she could only assume this must be the early hours of the morning. Strange, though, that she should be the only soul around. She would have expected stragglers heading home from the night-clubs, the occasional car at least. But except for her the place was deserted.

Mary reached a junction and halted, panting for breath. This was no good, she reasoned. Running about in the dark, carrying a small child. She could trip and fall if she wasn't careful, hurting Jessica in the process. She looked down at her baby. As their eyes met,the infant smiled and gurgled happily. Mary hugged the child tightly and started moving again, this time forcing herself to walk.

How she had come to be here was something she would worry about later. It could have been sunstroke. She had been out in the heat for hours. Or maybe someone in the camp had slipped her some drugs. Her mind, though, was a blank. No point in trying to fathom it. She had to get home as quickly as she could, for Jessica's sake. This was no time for an infant to be outdoors. She could catch her death.

Mary walked and walked until her feet ached, but could find no familiar landmark, just street after street of houses rendered indistinct by darkness. She could be in any city, in any part of the world. The absence of sound, of vehicles, of the merest indication of human presence, unnerved her. She felt close to tears. It was like being trapped in a bad dream. Maybe, Mary thought, she had been drugged after all.

She wished Kelvin was with her. He was level-headed, good in a crisis. Knowing him, he was probably frantic with worry, most likely had half the Swansea Police out scouring the city for her. Mary knew they hadn't been getting on, and was equally aware that it was her fault, not his. But he was a good man, a loving husband, and Mary

151

was certain it would be better between them now that they had their baby back.

Turning yet another corner, she was confronted by a high wall which stretched away in both directions as far as she could see. A warehouse, she guessed, craning her neck to look up towards the roof, which gleamed palely in the moonlight. She had been hoping to spot a sign or a painted name, anything to give her a clue as to where she was, but the building was as blank as her mind had been since her time in the camp. Mary's shoulders slumped. There was no way she could go on like this for much longer, not with the way her legs and arms hurt. Better, perhaps, to wait here until dawn, when hopefully there would be some people about and Mary could at least see where she was going. Except it would not be too long before Jessica became hungry and Mary had nothing, not even a piece of chocolate, to give her.

She stared at the warehouse again and saw something she had not noticed before. A few yards along the wall to the right of where she stood was a gap which divided the tiers of bricks, a narrow opening through which a light shone weakly. What she had thought of as a single building must in fact have been two, separated by a narrow lane. Curious, Mary crossed the road and approached it. As she drew nearer she thought she could hear distant traffic, which meant there were people around. Thank God for that, she thought, glad that she and her baby would be home soon.

But as she entered the lane, she was forced to step back as a crowd of people staggered past her. They were drunk by the looks of them, weaving and lurching and clutching bottles. Mary, afraid that a woman alone at this time of night could be in serious trouble, flattened herself against the wall in what she knew was a hopeless attempt to avoid being seen. The crowd, however, ignored her. She could not believe how many of them came out of the lane, men and women alike. Well over a hundred, maybe twice that, and not one of them making the slightest sound. After they had passed, Mary looked down the passage and saw a small figure illuminated by the streetlights around him. It was the boy from the camp. Standing next to him was a filthy-looking man with a wild beard who stared at Mary menacingly. Then she heard the boy's voice in her head as clearly as if the child stood right next to her.

Remember, he said. Mary did. Everything which had until now been a blank came back to her in a frantic rush of images. Kelvin taking her from the camp. Two others, a youth and a man, whom she did not recognise. The girl with the scarred face who had talked to her as soothingly as a mother would talk to a distraught child. Her flight through the streets, searching for the way out. No, she realised. That was not it.

She had been trying to find a way in.

You have done well, my Trojan Horse. Now join the others.

And that was the moment when Mary's world ended

The Ragchild

They swarmed through Old Town like a cancer, destroying its living heart from within. Petrol bombs crashed through windows at random. Fire spread quickly through the aged timbers until whole streets were ablaze. Their occupants either perished within or fled outside to apparent safety, only to have their lives snuffed out by the child's murderous army. The members of that army knew who they were looking for thanks to Mary's memories, and it was only a matter of time before they found her.

Captain watched with satisfaction as a corner shop erupted into flames. Its windows exploded with the intensity of the heat, the air around the building shimmering, alive with what looked like thousands of tiny fireflies. The shop door burst open and a woman ran out, screaming, hair and meagre clothes alight. She fell to the ground and thrashed about, continuing to moan deeply after extinguishing the flames which had engulfed her. Captain gave a hand signal and two of the child's followers stepped forward. One of them gripped the woman by the hair and pulled until her face was raised from the ground. Her screams became shriller. Captain swore loudly. It was not the one. The second follower bent over and twisted the woman's head. There was a sharp crack and she fell silent as her body went limp.

They moved on, Captain leading the way, indicating when he wanted one of the petrol bombs used. *We'll get the bitch. Just give us enough time and we'll have her.* But this time he was not talking to the child, only to himself. It was strange not to feel the boy's presence in his mind. He had almost grown used to it. But of course the child could not be with him, not here in the very stronghold of the enemy. That made no difference as far as Captain was concerned. The child trusted him. Captain knew what he had to do, and he was damn sure he would do it well. He had been so tantalisingly close to oblivion, there was no fucking way he would jeopardise it now.

To his left a house door opened and an old man looked out, weaving so badly that he had to lean against the frame for support. He had a bottle clasped in one hand which he raised to his lips before staggering back out of sight. Captain thought about torching the house, then had a better idea. Petrol bombs were effective enough, but they could spend all night using the fucking things and still not find the girl. No, what he needed was a different approach. He ordered the mob behind him to wait and walked towards the house. The door was unlocked. Captain opened it and stepped inside, pulling out a short but keen-edged knife. The place was in darkness so the old fucker could be hiding anywhere. No matter. Captain had time. The fire was already beginning to spread from rooftop to rooftop. It would not be long until entire neighbourhoods, let alone streets, went up in smoke.

He gripped the knife in his right hand at his side and held the left outstretched as he edged his way cautiously along the hall. In front of him he could see a narrow bar of flickering light on the floor. At first he thought the fire had shifted quicker than he'd anticipated, but then Captain decided otherwise. There was no smoke, no heat, no tell-tale crackle. He shuffled towards the light and his hand touched wood. A door. He felt around until his fingers brushed against a handle, which he turned. The door creaked open to reveal a small room, illuminated by candles and empty save for a table, chair and bed. The old man sat on the floor, back propped up against the wall, a whisky bottle at his lips. His eyes, when he looked up at Captain, were hooded, and his words when he spoke were so badly slurred they were almost incoherent. "And just who in God's name are you?" he demanded.

Captain said nothing. He stepped forward and slashed the knife across the back of the drunkard's hand. The man yelled and dropped the bottle to the floor. It smashed, sending glass skittering across the faded old carpet. The air suddenly reeked of whisky fumes. The old man clasped the wound with his good hand and tried to stagger to his feet. Captain, who by now was beginning to enjoy himself, kicked the old bastard down. "I need something from you," he said.

"Fuck off," the drunkard snapped back. "Who the hell do you -"

His words segued into a scream as Captain jabbed the blade into his cheek and ripped it down, feeling metal grate against bone. The old man put his hands to his face and slid to the floor. He lay there curled up like a foetus, groaning weakly, blood cascading through his fingers. Captain dropped to his knees and prodded the man's shoulder with the knife. "There's a girl," he said. "I need to know how to find her."

It was the one part of the child's strategy that had not worked out. He had told Captain the rough direction they needed to follow to reach the house Mary had been in. But she had run from it in darkness, taking turnings at random so that it was nigh on impossible to know exactly where the place was. Captain had two choices. He could either burn every last one of the bastards here out of their homes until he tracked down the girl, or he could find out from one of them where she lived. The second option had emerged as his favourite. It should not be too difficult. How many girls with scarred faces could there be in this fucking town? Apart from that, this option gave him the chance to inflict a little pain, and he was not one to turn down such opportunities.

So he spelled out what it was that he needed to know.

And when all he got in response was another feeble moan, Captain pulled the old man's hand away from his face and sliced off the first of his fingers.

Tom had never felt so hopeless in his life. Old Town, his home for so many years, was on fire and he did not know how or why. Neither did he know what he could do about it. As they neared the first of the burning buildings, the air became so thick with smoke that it was hard to breathe and even harder to see. It was like running through a dense fog, above which the sky glowed a sickly orange. For the first time since the war, Tom was afraid. This was definitely no accident. Someone, somehow, had managed to breach the town's defences with the obvious intention of destroying it.

He led Kelvin through the dark streets as quickly as conditions allowed, trusting to luck more than to his memory of Old Town's geography. Kelvin started calling out for Mary until Tom ordered him to stop. He sympathised with Kelvin and sincerely hoped they did find the missing woman, but their survival was foremost on his mind. Almost blinded, they had no idea who might be lurking nearby, and Tom did not want to make it easy for anyone with hostile intent to pin them down as a target.

One side of the street ahead of them was ablaze, flames rising high into the air and sending down a rain of burning embers. The scale of destruction was almost beyond Tom's comprehension. The only consolation was that the houses on the opposite side were intact, though how long they would remain so was anyone's guess. Tom stood in shocked silence, feeling nothing until the smoke began to sting his eyes. He coughed harshly, and took out a handkerchief which he pulled over his nose and mouth, knotting it at the back of his head. It helped, but not much. Tom glanced at Kelvin, who seemed just as confused and stunned by the carnage around them, then set off down the street, staying close to the unaffected buildings.

Transformed though it was by night and by flickering shadow, the place nevertheless seemed familiar to Tom. He tried hard to think where he was, but for a moment he couldn't focus his mind. Then he remembered. This was where Tinker lived. His friend's house was just a few yards away, intact for the time being, but the question was whether the old soak had already gotten out safely or was still inside, dead to the world, lost in a whisky-induced stupor. "Shit," Tom murmured. He did not want to stop, wanted to keep going until he found out who was starting the fires. But he could not leave unless he was sure Tinker was okay. He turned to Kelvin. "I've got to check something."

"What?"

"A friend of mine lives here. He might need our help."

Kelvin did not look happy. "Then we go and look for Mary, right?"

"Of course," Tom said, not feeling particularly guilty about the lie. The chances of them stumbling across Kelvin's wife in a town this size were remote. No, his main concern was Tinker, and then finding out what the hell was going on.

The front door was slightly ajar. Tom hoped that meant Tinker had left, and that all that would be needed would be a quick search of the house to confirm his absence. If he was there, drunk, they would have to carry him out, and that would slow them down. The sole light in the house came from the open door directly ahead of them. It was the only part of the building that Tinker used. Tom approached it, noticing the sour reek of whisky before he even reached it. He stepped into the room.

For a moment he failed to grasp exactly what he was seeing. Tinker was sprawled on the floor, shards of broken glass all around him. At first Tom thought he was asleep, drunk. That was before he saw the blood. It was all over Tinker's clothes and exposed flesh. Some of it had sprayed across the wall behind him, and it stained the carpet black where it had dripped from his supine body. His arms were flung out wide, and Tom felt dizzy when he caught sight of the mangled stumps where fingers had once been. "Sweet Jesus," he whispered, hearing Kelvin vomit noisily behind him and coming close to retching himself. He knelt by Tinker's body, cradled his friend's head in his arms. Tears welled up and he let them fall. "What have they done to you, old fella?" he said softly. "What have those bastards done to you, eh?"

Tinker's eyes flicked open, startling Tom. It seemed impossible that the old man could have survived such appalling injuries, yet somehow he had managed to keep a tentative hold on life. Blood ran from a deep gash in his cheek as his lips moved. No words emerged. Tinker coughed - a harsh, liquid cough which came from deep within his chest. Tom had heard that rattle too many times before, on the battlefield, and knew what it meant. "Take it easy," he said. "Don't try to talk."

"M-made me," Tinker said in an agonised croak. "Hurt me."

"Who did? Who did this to you?"

The Ragchild

Tinker shook his head. "They want ... Rhiannon."

The three words were his last. Tom felt Tinker's body slump, saw the light go out of his eyes. Martyn had asked what would happen if someone was killed in Old Town. Now Tom knew the answer. They stayed dead. He lowered the man's head gently to the floor and stood, trembling with rage. Nobody deserved to die in such a brutal way, least of all a friend. He reined his anger in. Revenge had to wait. Someone was after Rhiannon, for whatever reason, and Tom knew he must reach her first.

Captain ran ahead of the child's followers, eager to finish his work. He carried one of the petrol bombs, which he would use only if the girl proved too hard to handle. That old bastard had been a hard nut to crack, but he had given in eventually. Now the end was in sight. All he had to do was get to the bitch and kill her. Then Captain would have done all that the child had asked of him, and oblivion would be his forever.

He arrived at the street he was looking for, searched out the door number. When he found it he paused to catch his breath. He put down the petrol-filled bottle, deciding he preferred the personal touch, then took the knife from his pocket. Captain gazed almost lovingly at the blood-encrusted blade. It would get bloodier still before this night was over. Smiling to himself, he kicked the door open and went in.

Martyn stood at the window, tense with frustration as he watched the fire edge closer. He was furious with Tom for ordering him to stay behind. Of course, Tom had made out that Martyn would be doing him a favour by taking care of Rhiannon. But the truth was, he just didn't want Martyn in his way. That was so obvious he might just as well have come right out and said it. So here Martyn was, pacing the room nervously, when he he believed should be out there on the streets at least trying to do something to help. Rhiannon, after all, was older than him and could look after herself. In fact, she was so grateful that he was here to take care of her that she had crept off into one of the other rooms, leaving him alone. Thanks a bunch, he thought sourly.

Staring out at the glowing sky, he felt suddenly guilty over his resentment of Tom. It was almost certainly too dangerous out there for him to have allowed Martyn to leave the house. There was nothing to be done now except wait and hope Tom was okay. Kelvin, too. Martyn felt sorry for him, losing his daughter and now his wife.

He decided to check on Rhiannon. She had been strangely quiet since the two men had left. She was never a talkative person, but on the other hand she was never rude. Which is why it was odd for her to have walked out without a word. Maybe she was ill. Martyn found her in the room where he had recovered after his beating. She was curled up on the bed, eyes closed. Even in the dim candlelight he could see her forehead was slick with sweat. As he approached her, she began to moan quietly. Her body juddered. He considered waking her, and then he remembered that sleep was not a necessity in Old Town. She really must be sick, and Martyn had no idea how to deal with it. He wished Tom would hurry back. Surely he would know what to do.

With a gasp, Rhiannon sat bolt upright, breathing hard. Her eyes were wide, and though she looked at Martyn she did not appear to see him.

"We have to leave," she said. "We have to leave *now*."

The stairwell was unlit and Captain took his time ascending, not wanting to stumble or make the slightest noise which would alert his prey. It was a struggle, because he really wanted to find the bitch and deal with her in his own sweet way. Maybe he'd treat himself to a fuck, just before he finished her off with the blade. The girl in the camp had whetted his appetite for sex. Then again, maybe he would just use the knife and get the hell out of there. The place was fucking weird. Besides, oblivion would be his reward once his work was over, and he did not want to keep it waiting.

Remembering with perfect clarity everything Mary had seen, Captain had no problem finding the door to the girl's apartment. He expected it to be locked, but it swung open quietly when he turned the handle. Tightening his grip on the knife, he stepped inside and waited until his eyes adjusted to the candlelight which, soft as it was, dazzled him after the darkness of the stairs. He was in a long corridor studded with doorways on both sides. Captain crept forward and eased into the first of the rooms. It was empty. No matter. It was merely a question of being patient while he searched the rest of the rooms in turn. He would find her eventually, and he had plenty of time.

But within a matter of minutes he was not so certain. There was no sign of her anywhere. The place was deserted, he was sure. Fuck it. Captain sat down on a chair next to the window, glancing outside long enough to admire the effects of his own handiwork. The whole fucking town looked alight, and he even thought he could smell the smoke. He had done his job well, oh yes indeed, which would please the child no end. However, the child would not be pleased at all if Captain failed to kill the girl, a mistake he had no intention of making. He dreaded to think how he might be made to pay for it. He pondered his options. One was to go back outside and carry on the search as before, except that could take forever if the girl had decided to hide. Or he could wait here in the hope that she would return once she thought the danger had passed. Yes, that was the better of the two. It had been a busy day and he was fucking bushed. Might as well grab some rest while he could. Captain relaxed back in the chair and absently scraped beneath his fingernails with the blade.

Which was when he heard the sound of soft footsteps coming from the hallway.

Tom did not stop running until he saw the mob ahead. They shuffled along the street in ghostly silence, a few clutching bottles which had rags stuffed into the necks. Must be a couple of hundred of them at least, Tom guessed, despairing. If there had been a handful to deal with he could have held his own in a scrap. But not against this many. He would have to circle around via the side streets to get past them. That meant wasting time, time he did not have to spare. Every second that was lost brought Rhiannon closer to harm.

Kelvin stumbled to a halt beside him, breathing harshly, bending to put his hands on his knees. "F-friends of yours?" he panted, glancing up at the mob.

Tom shook his head. "Trouble."

"Yeah, I'd sort of worked that out for myself. What now?"

"Sneak around them," Tom said. "Pray we get to Rhiannon before they do."

Tom half-expected the other man to balk, to insist that they continue the search for his wife. Which was unfair, really. Kelvin had not hesitated when Tom ran from Tinker's house, and he did not protest now. He may have been in dubious shape for a man of his age, but he was not lacking in guts. "Better get a move on," he said.

They turned left, then right, so that they were running parallel to the mob. When Tom estimated they had gone far enough to be safe, he led Kelvin right and left, then slowed before they re-emerged onto the street they had detoured from. He peered around the corner; the shuffling gang were not as far behind as he had hoped, but he supposed the distance between them would suffice. He nodded at Kelvin, then sprinted down the road without a backward glance, shoulders tensed, expecting a hail of burning bottles to explode around him, or at the very least a yell to indicate they had been spotted. But there was nothing save their ragged breathing and the pounding of their feet. Almost there, he thought. Please, God, please let her still be safe.

When he reached the house, it looked as though his prayer had been answered. The place seemed fine, no sign of any fire, the front door closed, just as he'd left it. But then he drew closer and saw the bottle which had been placed on the ground. Tom felt a sick cold dread as he realised he was too late. He turned to Kelvin. "Stay here," he said. "I'm going to try to get Rhiannon out of the house. If you see her, grab her and run. Keep going, d'you hear me? Don't stop for anything."

"Wait —" Kelvin said, his voice cut off as the door behind him, the one next to where Rhiannon lived, crashed open and a figure lunged out at them. Tom stepped forward, fists up, ready to start throwing punches, when he recognised their assailant as Martyn. Rhiannon emerged more cautiously after him. At the sight of her, Tom's shock turned to overwhelming relief. He threw one arm around Martyn, the other around Rhiannon, pulling them close to disguise the fact that he was trembling.

"What the hell were you two doing in there?" he said.

Martyn eased away from Tom's embrace, visibly embarrassed. "Hiding. Rhiannon said we had to leave right away. When we got down, this man was running towards us. You know, the bearded one. The one who killed Kelvin's friend. I managed to drag Rhiannon into the house next door before he could see us."

Kelvin looked up sharply. "How long ago was this?"

"Couple of minutes, that's all."

"That means he's still in there," Kelvin said grimly. "I owe that bastard one."

"Forget him," Martyn said, glancing nervously down the street. "Let the police deal with him later. We have to get out of here before his friends catch up."

"The boy's right," Tom said.

"No," Rhiannon said, surprising him. "This is where it ends."

Tom frowned. "What are you talking about?"

"Everything is in place, Tom. Now the last moves must be played out."

"I don't understand."

Rhiannon's eyes closed briefly as if in pain. Her voice sounded immeasurably sad. "Sometimes the distance between two places is not quite as far as it seems."

Tom, stunned, his mind reaching back more than eighty years, vividly recalled the words of the stranger on the battlefield, the words that Rhiannon could not possibly have known. He had not told her about that inexplicable encounter - had not told anyone, come to that—

165

although the memory, unlike the bullet, had left a scar which had never properly healed. Yet she did know the words. And when she leaned forward and kissed Tom, he understood why. He understood everything there was to know.

Because Rhiannon was not human. She was a construct of Old Town, the living personification of its essence, created to protect it from the destruction it now faced. The buildings would burn but Old Town would live, could heal itself later, so long as Rhiannon survived. Tom saw it all in an instant. The force which fed on souls, appearing as a boy because, ancient though it may be, it was a mere child compared to eternity, and because the guise made it seem less of a threat. It was not a physical entity, but it was cunning and utterly without pity, promising its victims whatever they most desired in return for their immortal souls. And then it owned them, maintained them as an army of soulless puppets to suit its own purposes. For now it hungered for more than human prey. It was after the greatest prize there could be. The soul of the living city.

Tom felt as if he were floating on air, looking down as the German bombs tore Swansea apart. Now he knew why Rhiannon, otherwise perfect, was blighted with scars. They were a representation of the awesome damage inflicted during the Blitz. He saw the city resurrect itself brick by brick, tile by tile, paving stone by paving stone, in a secret realm, a place beyond the here and now. It could be anywhere, at any time. For it, the distance between two places, between two moments in history, was no distance at all. It had always known this moment would come, and had prepared for it. Old Town had reached back to the Great War, sacrificing part of itself to the soul-eater in order to save the life of Thomas Vaughan, knowing he would one day be the instrument of its salvation.

When the moment drew near, Old Town and the child gathered their forces and moved them into place. There had been no coincidences, as Tom had suspected, only skirmishes as each side tested the other's strategy and mettle. They had been so evenly matched until the child's master stroke: sending Mary back with them, the memory of her surrender to the boy buried so deep that Old Town's defences had been deceived. It was Mary who had opened the way, and Tom's preordained role was to heal the breach. He should have died on that battlefield, but Old Town had intervened, giving him eighty years which by rights should not have been his. Now it was time to pay back the debt. Tom knew what he had to do, and it terrified him.

He blinked and looked at Rhiannon, who looked back unsmiling. Tom turned to face Martyn. "Listen," he said. "I want you and Kelvin to get Rhiannon out of here. I don't know where you should take her. Just keep going. Keep her safe, all right?"

"What about you? You can't take on that many people."

"Don't need to, lad. Cut off the head and the body dies." Martyn looked hopelessly confused. Tom reached out and gripped his arm. "The bearded man. He's the only one whose soul is his own. Without him the child is powerless here."

Martyn glanced up at the house. "Don't go in there, Tom. Come with us."

"I want to," Tom sighed. "More than anything. But I have to do this."

He took a step towards the house, then hesitated. Reaching under his shirt, Tom unclipped the chain from around his neck and held the St Christopher's medal out to Martyn. "Look after this for me, would you, lad? I'd hate to lose it."

"Sure." Martyn reached for the medal. Their hands clasped and the boy's eyes shone. "As long as you don't expect me to hold on to it for too long."

He knows, Tom thought. *Of course he knows*. He tried to speak but the words caught in his throat. Instead he smiled, raised an arm in farewell and, not daring to look back in case he changed his mind, stepped lightly to the door. He pushed it open, standing well back and to the side in case the bearded man was waiting to spring out at him. The hallway was in darkness and, at first glance, appeared empty. Tom reached into his pocket for his lighter, then remembered the petrol bomb which had been left outside the house. Retrieving it, he then flicked the lighter with his free hand. The flame was feeble but sufficient to guide him as he stepped inside the house, elbowing the door shut. Tom halted at the foot of the stairs, placing the petrol bomb on one of the steps before him. He pulled out his Woodbines and lit one, leaning casually against the wall, inhaling the smoke deeply, savouring it, the condemned man determined to enjoy his last cigarette. When it had all but vanished, Tom dropped it to the floor and reached down for the bottle. He took the first half-dozen or so stairs at a trot, then paused while he lit the rag before tossing the bomb down to the hallway. The sound of glass shattering was quickly subsumed by a sudden *whoomph,* and a searing explosion of flame. Tom grinned. No way out.

He took the stairs quickly, feeling the heat on the back of his neck and hearing a resounding series of cracks as the old timber was rapidly consumed. Thick black smoke billowed up the stairwell, yet even though his eyes were streaming Tom could see that Rhiannon's door was open. He felt around in his pocket, wishing he had something he could use as a weapon. There was nothing except his cigarettes, some loose change and the lighter. Ah well. If it was a fight that Captain fella was after, then that was what he would get. The old-fashioned, bare-knuckled type. Tom looked behind him, saw orange flames lick over the uppermost edge of the banisters. No time left to prevaricate. He sighed, stepped through the doorway. There was no sound, no sign of life, but Tom knew Captain was there. He even knew which room he was in, so that was where Tom headed, as quietly as he could, not wanting to give the other man the slightest advantage. Just before he reached the door, a figure burst out, raised arm swinging wildly. Tom blocked the punch effortlessly, realising too late that he had been duped. Captain's other arm darted up and something cold and sharp plunged deep into Tom's guts. There was no pain, just a freezing numbness, and Tom knew he had been stabbed. The world turned a hazy grey. Tom felt himself falling.

He must have blanked out momentarily, for the next thing he knew Captain was crouched over him, face split by an evil grin. "Been waiting a long time for this moment," the bearded man said, his breath a wave of foulness. "Got a score to settle with you, oh yes. Pity you couldn't put up more of a fucking fight, but there you go."

"This isn't over yet," Tom said, surprising himself with the strength of his own voice. Before Captain had a chance to move, Tom jackknifed his knee upwards, feeling it connect solidly with the man's balls. Captain grunted deep and harsh and lashed out with the knife. The blade sliced thin air. Tom rolled over, then used the doorframe to pull himself up. Captain was bent over, the floor below him glistening with vomit, and Tom kicked at his downturned face. His boot connected with sufficient force to hurl Captain against the wall. But it did not stop him. With a roar he bounded to his feet and stalked towards Tom, slashing left and then right as he advanced. Tom backed into the room and grabbed one of the candleholders. It was metal and just long enough for him to use to parry the knife. But Captain face, his face a mask of fury, wielded the blade with such savage strength that Tom knew he could not hold out much longer. He still felt no pain but he was tiring fast, and a quick glance down confirmed his shirt was awash with dark blood.

"Gonna fucking-well open you up," Captain snarled. "Gonna finish you off nice and fucking slow, then I'm going after that bitch friend of yours, oh yes indeed."

"Is that right," Tom said, as nonchalantly as he could manage.

"You bet your fucking life on it -"

Captain's words were drowned out by a booming roar as flames rushed down the narrow corridor, sucking deeply at the air. His eyes widened as he saw what was happening. Tom smiled at him. "You're not going anywhere, my friend," he said.

"We'll see about that," Captain snapped back, jabbing his fist forward. The knife caught the edge of the candleholder and scraped along it until it sliced deep into Tom's knuckles, forcing him to relinquish his grip. Again there was no pain, but even so Tom could not raise his hand fast enough to counter the punch Captain threw at him. It caught Tom squarely on the chin, and he tumbled to the floor with sufficient force to drive the air from his lungs. As if from far away, he saw Captain pick up one of the chairs and raise it high above his head. Tom closed his eyes, knowing this was the end and not wanting to see it. Shattering glass made him open them again, and he realised what Captain was doing. He had thrown the chair through the window and was levering himself up onto the sill, no doubt having figured out that jumping from the building offered a better chance of survival than remaining inside it. The fire crackled and spat in the corridor. Slender orange fingers curled around the doorframe as if tentatively feeling the way. The wallpaper next to the frame scorched, then smouldered, then finally erupted into flame. Tom was in no doubt that if he did not move quickly, he would never move again.

He forced himself to his knees, then slowly stood, swaying as the room spun around him. Coughing from the acrid smoke, he staggered across to the window, reaching it just as Captain was about to jump. Tom grabbed the bearded man around his waist and hauled backwards. For one heart-stopping moment he thought Captain's superior strength would win out, but then the two of them were falling backwards, the knife skittering from Captain's hands as he crashed to the floor. Tom, who had the element of surprise on his side, was the first to recover. He rolled over and slammed his fist into his opponent's midriff. Air burst explosively from Captain's lips. Tom pushed himself upright and groped around on the carpet until his fingers closed on the candleholder. He had been trying to find the knife in the smoke-filled room, but this would have to do. Tom raised it, but his wrist was clasped with bone-crunching strength and Captain's black-streaked face pushed into his. "You can't fucking stop me," he spat.

"Too late for that, laddie," Tom said, jerking his head back and then snapping it forward, feeling Captain's nose break with a great deal of satisfaction. The bearded man roared and grabbed at him, seizing Tom in a bear-hug so tight he could hardly breathe. Tom's ribs

171

screamed at him. He tried to break free, but the blood loss had left him too weak. It didn't matter. All Tom had to do was keep Captain occupied for just a few more minutes. He had felt the heat through the floorboards beneath him when he fell, and reckoned the fire must have become a raging inferno on the floor below by now. They were almost at the end. He was not afraid. Wood creaked and snapped beneath them. Sad, yes, but not afraid. He would never walk in Old Town again, would never breathe in its clean air or taint his lungs with another Woodbine. Worst of all, he would never see Rhiannon again, or Martyn.

The floor gave way and they fell into flame. Captain screamed as his flesh blackened and shrivelled. Tom felt nothing. It was, he knew, Old Town's parting gift to him. Just because he had to die did not mean he had to die in agony. He wished he could have one more cigarette. Then he realised he was already smoking.

When the end came, Tom was laughing.

Martyn's every instinct told him to run, but he made himself hold back. If there came the slightest sign that the mob posed any threat, then he would take off. But for the moment, at least, they did not appear interested in Martyn and his companions. Once they reached Rhiannon's house they stopped and stood there motionless, as if they had no idea what to do. Maybe they didn't, Martyn thought. Maybe they could not think for themselves, could do nothing unless the bearded man told them.

He watched in silence from a few dozen yards down the street, stomach tight with tension, willing Tom to get out of the house before the fire really caught hold. One of the ground-floor windows suddenly exploded outwards. Flames and black smoke boiled out into the night. Beside him, Rhiannon gave a sudden gasp and grabbed Martyn's arm, her fingers digging in so deep that he almost cried out in pain.

Then he heard her weep and he knew that Tom was dead. It hurt more than he ever could have imagined, hurt more than when Mum had died, maybe because he was older now and understood that death was the end. The realisation that he had lost his friend, the man to whom he owed his life, hit him like a knockout blow. But he had no time to grieve. A moment after he heard Rhiannon weep, he was knocked to his knees by a roar so earth-shatteringly loud that he thought his head would split. Martyn clapped his hands to his ears and squeezed. The pain in his skull was unimaginable. The buildings around him seemed to vibrate as if they were being rocked by an earthquake. Through tear-filled eyes he could see that Kelvin, too, was holding his head in obvious agony. Rhiannon, though, merely stood there as if nothing was happening. Then the noise stopped abruptly, and Martyn almost sobbed with relief. He wiped at his eyes, sniffing. Rhiannon said something to him, but the ringing in Martyn's head drowned out the words. She spoke again, voice raised.

"Look," she said, pointing up the street.

Martyn turned just in time to see the mob, every single man and woman, collapse to the ground as one, like puppets whose strings had been cut. They lay where they had fallen, unmoving, Martyn blinked and shook his head, frowning at Rhiannon. "I don't get it," he said. "What happened?"

"We won." She smiled, but the smile quickly faltered and she looked down. "Tom," she whispered, just loud enough for Martyn to hear. "I'm so sorry."

173

The Ragchild

It was the first time he had seen Mary look peaceful since Jessica was taken. Even the fine lines around her eyes and mouth had been smoothed out. Kelvin held her in his arms and rocked her gently, willing her to look at him, to say something, anything, willing her to breathe. But she would not. Of course she would not, a voice in his head told him. She was dead. He had searched for her and had found her, after turning over a dozen or more bodies. Despite the evidence to the contrary, Kelvin had been convinced she was alive. Everything that had happened, the rows, the arguments, all of that was forgotten. He just wanted Mary back. But seeing her there, face slack, arms wide, was enough to make him wish he had not found her after all. At least then he could pretend she was out there somewhere, still alive, like his daughter, and that one day all three of them would be together again. But that voice, that uncaring fucking voice in his head, just kept repeating the same two words over and over. *She's dead. She's dead. She's dead.* Kelvin wasn't even sure who *she* was meant to be. It could be Tanya, or Jessica, or Mary. He had lost the three of them, after all. Had lost everything that ever mattered to him.

He barely felt Rhiannon's hand on his shoulder.

"No," she said softly. "Not everything."

- CODA -

- i -

Healing the Wounds

All he could recall of the rest of that night was a series of fragmented images. Rhiannon taking Mary from him, placing her gently on the ground before helping him to his feet. Being inside a building of some kind. Martyn asking him if he was okay. It was then that Kelvin had blacked out. Had slept twelve hours straight, even though they had told him there was no need for sleep in Old Town. When he woke he was in a room he had never seen before, empty save for the bed on which he lay. When the events of the previous night flooded back the grief came too, crippling him. He felt worse than he had when he'd found Mary's body.

That had been three days ago. It still hurt, but not as deeply, and now at least he was back home.

"Try not to let it get you down. She'll turn up before long, don't you worry."

Kelvin's face must have betrayed his emotions. "Sorry?"

"Keep your spirits up," Miles said. "I'm sure Mary will be home soon."

Kelvin glanced at the detective, managed a wan smile, looked away. He knew Miles meant well, but the truth was that Mary would never be coming home. Even if Kelvin had wanted to bring her body out with him, he couldn't have. It had gone, along with the corpses of those who had died with her. They had, quite literally, vanished overnight. By the time Kelvin was fit enough to go outside, the street was empty. Most of the fire-damaged buildings around him had already regenerated. It was as if everything that had happened was nothing more than a bad dream.

There were so many questions he wanted to ask, but Rhiannon told him they must wait. She and Martyn had work to do, she said. So did Kelvin. When he asked what she meant, Rhiannon told him to go home and wait for the police to call.

"I hope you don't mind me stopping off unannounced," said Miles.

"Not at all," Kelvin said. He noticed the detective's empty glass. "Another?"

"Better not. Thanks anyway, but one whisky's enough. I'm still on duty."

"Some other time," Kelvin said, knowing there would be other times. As far as Miles was concerned, Mary was missing but not presumed dead. The theory he had shared with Kelvin was that she had linked up with the people at Morfa and had left Swansea with them. But Miles was convinced she would grow tired of their company. Which was why he had gone to town with the publicity for the other big breakthrough, the one that had even the national press interested. Miles was hoping Mary would hear what had happened and come straight back home.

The catalyst had been a single, anonymous phone call.

Which Martyn had made.

Miles put the glass down and stood. "Well, I'd better be off."

"Thanks for calling," Kelvin said, also rising. "I appreciate it."

More than you'll ever know, he thought, remembering how

Miles had come around to break the news in person. The tip-off had been solid. They had found her in a council flat in Clase, in the care of a young girl who'd miscarried after four months and never recovered from it. Kelvin refused to press charges. The girl needed help, not punishment, and besides, she had looked after the little one well.

Behind him, through the intercom, he could hear Jessica start to cry.

"I reckon your daughter needs you." Miles was smiling.

"Yes," Kelvin said, adding silently: *But not as much as I need her.*

A Man of Two Worlds

Martyn stood at the window, staring out at Old Town without really seeing it. He was trying, and failing, to make some kind of sense out of what had happened.

Rhiannon had withdrawn into herself during the three days that had passed since Tom's death. Martyn could understand that. He too still grieved for his friend, and since Rhiannon had known Tom a lot longer, the sadness must be all the more intense for her.But their grief was the only real change; there were no visible signs in Old Town of what had happened. Everything had gone back to the way it had been before the night of the fires. By dawn of the following morning the buildings had restored themselves. The corpses in the street were gone. To Martyn, it felt as if time had run backwards. If only Tom was there to complete the illusion, he thought, and briefly closed his eyes.

From the few short conversations he'd had with Rhiannon, Martyn had been able to figure out at least part of what it had all been about. He understood that the soul-eater had been unable to enter Old Town and so have direct control over its army. Instead it it had entrusted them to Captain. Why the soul-eater had targeted Rhiannon was something Martyn had not yet discovered. It might have had something to do with her healing powers, he supposed, though he had no idea what or why. She certainly had not been able to do anything for all those people who had died, Tom included. Martyn sighed. Perhaps he would find out one day. The one thing he was sure of, because he had witnessed it himself, was that once Captain had perished, the threat to Old Town was over. Whether the soul-eater had killed its followers in a fit of rage, or whether they were dead from the moment they succumbed to its powers, was something else Martyn doubted he would ever know. Not that it mattered. They were gone. End of story.

He fingered the St Christopher's medal around his neck, contemplating his own future. Martyn had left Old Town just the once, to telephone the police. He had written down the address Rhiannon had told him on a scrap of paper, reading it out from the kiosk and replacing the receiver when the girl who answered his 999 call started asking questions. Then he had come straight back, not sure if he ever wanted to leave again. Old Town was safe. It felt more like home than Swansea did.

The paper was still in his pocket. Martyn pulled it out and studied it, hoping the information was correct and wondering how on earth Rhiannon could have known if it was. Kelvin had promised to bring his daughter to them if she was returned to him, and after all the fuss had settled down, but there was no sign of him yet.

Rhiannon knew things, Tom had told him. Martyn wanted to believe that.

Because maybe then she could explain what his role in all this had been. It seemed to him that he, like Kelvin, had been caught up in events rather than having any significant part to play in them. The key roles had been filled by Tom and Rhiannon on the one side, and Captain and Mary on the other. It angered him that his world had been so drastically changed, that he had been through so much pain, and it had all been for nothing.

"Don't feel bitter," Rhiannon said from behind, startling him. He had not heard her enter the room. They were back in her flat, which looked no different to the way it had before the fire. Even the furniture was intact.

Martyn could not bring himself to face her. "Why not?"

"You do have a part to play. Maybe the most important one of all now."

"Yeah, sure," he sighed, hearing her soft footsteps on the carpet as she crossed the room to him. When she placed her hands on his shoulders, he shuddered. Her touch was electric. It helped Martyn understand everything. He knew they had only stopped the child, not beaten it. There would come a day when it would return. Maybe it would move on elsewhere in the meantime, find some other city's secret inner self and gorge itself on that. But it would be back. Old Town knew that, just like it knew everything else. It had organised its defences well for the first attack, but they had been battered and now it had to rebuild them. Which was where Martyn came in. He would, like Tom before him, be a man of two worlds. The difference was that, whereas Tom's journeys had been purely for the sake of curiosity and commerce, Martyn's task was to search the streets of Swansea, to look for others like himself and bring them into Old Town. Their vitality was necessary to help heal the ravages the soul-eater had inflicted. And they would be ready and waiting for the day it returned.

When that happened, Old Town would have an army of its own.

There was more. Something about Rhiannon, something important, but the contact between them was broken before Martyn could see what. He gasped and rocked on his heels. Old Town had been in his head, and he had never felt anything like it in his life. He had only glimpsed a fraction of its power, but even that was enough to tell him that the forces at work here were too awesome to comprehend. And now he was a part of it, as much as it was a part of him.

"When do I start?" he asked.

Also available from RazorBlade Press:

razorblades
edited by Darren Floyd
ISBN: 0-9531468-0-4 £3.99 144pgs

Faith in the Flesh
by Tim Lebbon
ISBN: 0-9531468-4-7 £4.99/$9.00 144pgs

The Dreaming Pool
by Gary Greenwood
ISBN: 0-9531468-7-1 £4.99/$9.00 136pgs

Lonesome Roads
by Peter Crowther
ISBN: 0-9531468-1-2 £5.99/$13.99 154pgs

Hideous Progeny
Edited by Brian Willis
ISBN 0-9531468 4 1 £6.99/$11.00 310pgs

coming soon:
Hush
by Tim Lebbon & Gavin Williams
ISBN: 0-9531468-2-1 £8.99/$13.00

For more information about RazorBlade Press
visit our website at:

www.razorbladepress.com